GO SLOWLY. DON'T LOOK DOWN.

I moved to the edge of the ravine. .... e its bottom, for it was dark as the netherworld. First I tested the board lightly with one foot, then I stepped onto it sideways, moving along it like a river crab. Not daring to look down, I went very, very slowly. I moved one foot out to the side and then steadily brought the other foot up next to it. I heard Dovid's derisive laugh at my method, but it seemed far away, as in a dream. Step, step, step . . . one foot beside the other. A cracking sound! Pay no attention, I told myself. You have to go on. Go on. Go on. Go slowly, I repeated silently. Don't look down.

How much farther to go? Not much. Ignore Dovid. Ignore him! Keep going. One step and another and then—I felt it! The familiar feel of soil under my left foot. I brought my right foot to meet it. I had crossed the ravine.

When I turned to look back, I saw in the fading light Dovid stepping out onto the plank. He went across it slowly, facing forward. Suddenly a volley of noise cut through the night. GUNFIRE!

OTHER PUFFIN BOOKS YOU MAY ENJOY

Anna Is Still Here   Ida Vos

Becoming Gershona   Nava Semel

Days of Awe   Kimmel/Weihs

The Devil in Vienna   Doris Orgel

The Devil's Arithmetic   Jane Yolen

Escape from Egypt   Sonia Levitin

Friedrich   Hans Peter Richter

Grace in the Wilderness   Aranka Siegal

Hide and Seek   Ida Vos

The House on Walenska Street   Charlotte Herman

I Am a Star   Inge Auerbacher

Letters from Rifka   Karen Hesse

Lydia, Queen of Palestine   Uri Orlev

Mischling, Second Degree   Ilse Koehn

The Night Journey   Kathryn Lasky

A Pocket Full of Seeds   Marilyn Sachs

The Rabbi's Girls   Johanna Hurwitz

To Cross a Line   Karen Ray

To Life   Ruth Minsky Sender

Touch Wood   Renee Roth-Hano

Upon the Head of the Goat   Aranka Siegal

The
CIRCLEMAKER

MAXINE ROSE SCHUR

PUFFIN BOOKS

PUFFIN BOOKS

Published by the Penguin Group

Penguin Books USA Inc., 375 Hudson Street, New York, New York 10014, U.S.A.

Penguin Books Ltd, 27 Wrights Lane, London W8 5TZ, England

Penguin Books Australia Ltd, Ringwood, Victoria, Australia

Penguin Books Canada Ltd, 10 Alcorn Avenue, Toronto, Ontario, Canada M4V 3B2

Penguin Books (N.Z.) Ltd, 182–190 Wairau Road, Auckland 10, New Zealand

Penguin Books Ltd, Registered Offices: Harmondsworth, Middlesex, England

First published in the United States of America by Dial Books for Young Readers,
a division of Penguin Books USA Inc., 1994
Published in Puffin Books, 1996

7 9 10 8

THE LIBRARY OF CONGRESS HAS CATALOGED THE DIAL EDITION AS FOLLOWS:
Schur, Maxine.
The circlemaker / by Maxine Rose Schur.—1st ed.
p. cm.
Summary: In mid-nineteenth-century Russia, Mendel Cholinsky, a
twelve-year-old Jewish boy, tries to escape to America to avoid being
taken into the czar's army for twenty-five years of military service.
ISBN 0-8037-1354-1
[1. Jews—Russia—Fiction. 2. Runaways—Fiction. 3. Russia—Fiction.]
I. Title. II. Title: Circlemaker.
PZ7.S3964Ci 1994 [Fic]—dc20 93-17983 CIP AC

This book was made possible, in part, by a grant from
The Society of Children's Book Writers.

Though some of the incidents in this book are based on actual historical reports, the
characters are entirely fictional, as are many of the towns and villages.
—Maxine Rose Schur

Puffin Books ISBN 0-14-037997-5

Printed in the United States of America

For my son, Ethan

MOLOVSK, UKRAINE

THE PALE OF SETTLEMENT

APRIL 24, 1852

———————————

The Pale of Settlement consisted of twenty-five provinces of czarist Russia to which Jews were restricted to live. The Pale was created in 1791 and abolished in 1917.

1

As soon as I woke, I knew it would be only minutes until day. I lay under my covers and waited. Sure enough, soon the broken window over my bed showed the moon fade into a paling sky. This was my favorite time—when my village lay trapped between the dark and the light. For a brief, beautiful moment the dawn of the new day was like the dusk of the past one. Quickly I threw off my blankets and jumped onto the flax mat over our dirt floor. I said my prayers and in the tin bowl washed my fingers clean of any bad night spirits that may have rested on them while I slept. Then I got dressed.

Behind the hanging blanket that separated my bed from the one in which my mother and father slept, I wrapped the prayer shawl around my waist and put on my shirt. First I buttoned the third and fifth buttons and then went back up and buttoned the second, first, and fourth buttons. I knew well that the Evil Eye loves to hide in clothes but cannot enter a garment that is irregularly buttoned. I pulled on my breeches, buttoning the middle button first, then the top button, then the bottom one.

With the Evil Eye a person can never be too careful.

Though my parents were asleep, our hut was noisy. My mother slept quietly, but my father snored. With each snore the rusty bed let out squeaks and wheezes, so it always seemed to me as if both Papa and bed were snoring together.

I had to be careful now, for if I woke my parents, they'd ask their questions. I curled my earlocks with spit, stuck on my cap, and tiptoed to the shelf. I found a roll . . . not too stale. I spread a thin layer of goat cheese on it, stuffed it into my pocket, then slowly and very quietly moved toward the door.

"Mendel! Again you are up so early!"

I turned and saw my mother standing by her bed. She was tall as a man but thin, and her hair, curly and red like my own, poked out from the dark-blue *babushka* she wore even when she slept.

"Yes, Mama, I'm going out."

"Out? So, where can you go at this hour? Often you leave before we even wake! The day has just been hatched and you are running out!"

"I like to walk early. I need the time to think about things. . . ."

"Things?"

"Yes, Mama. The great questions asked by Rashi, Rabbi Akiba, and . . . uh . . . Moses Maimonides."

As I spoke, I looked down at my shoes, for whenever I lied I could not look into my mother's dark eyes.

My mother sighed. "All right, Mendel, walk. But don't be late for school."

"I won't."

"And no dawdling. Do not be tempted to play with your shadow or walk on the cracks of Volminsky Street. It is the dark hidden places where the Evil Eye lurks."

"I know," I said, turning to the door.

She grabbed my hand and pulled it back, holding me firmly.

"Above all," she said, "don't talk to the peasants. Do not torment their animals; do not whisper behind their backs or look into their eyes. And do not answer any of their questions. Not a word, Mendel!"

"Yes, Mama."

My mother looked down at me with worried eyes. I stretched up to plant a quick kiss on her hollow cheek, and hurried outside.

2

Outside! Outside the air was as clear and cold as river water. I ran fast. Down the graveyard hill from my home—past the first row of crooked wooden huts toward school. But when I knew my mother could no longer see me, I changed direction and ran toward the river.

I ran the way I loved to run—more like flying! My feet leapt off the ground, and my earlocks fluttered in the wind, tickling my cheeks. It's true I was thin for my age. Sometimes other boys called me "Noodle Legs," but I didn't care. I could run faster and jump higher than any of them.

"Out of the way!" I yelled at the stray chickens as I hopped over the slop gullies. I sprinted around Zenvil the Knife Sharpener's tiny hut. I raced past the filthy hut of the Ragpicker, whose son Dovid was the meanest boy I knew. Their hut was stuffed with rags to keep out the wind. Zalman called Dovid "Rag Rat." Zalman! Just thinking of my best friend made me run faster. I ran and ran through the twisted up-and-down streets of my village until I came to the very end—at Meyer the Water Carrier's hut. To the left curled a path leading down to the Dniester. Down I raced. But when I reached the riverbank, I saw that Zalman wasn't there!

Zalman had always been there waiting for me. Ever since we'd made a pact to meet secretly every Sunday morning before school.

I paced up and down the riverbank . . . no one in sight.

I picked up a rock and flung it hard into the river.

Boiled fish! I thought. What good is a friend if you can't depend on him?

I threw more rocks into the water, and when I got tired of that, I sat under the big pine tree and waited.

CRACK! A pebble bounced off my head.

I looked around, as that was just the kind of trick Zalman played. But I saw no one.

SMACK! A small pinecone dropped on my shoulder. I looked up into the tree, trying to spot a squirrel moving in the branches, but the branches were so thick with needles I could see nothing.

CRACK! Another pebble grazed my ear.

I jumped up quickly, just in time to avoid an avalanche of cones and pebbles. Then I heard:

Bom Tshi-tshe!
Bom Tshi-tshe!
Khaseme Feygele!
Gibmir a chitkele lekach!

Bom Tshi-tshe!
Bom Tshi-tshe!
Wedding Birdie!
Give me a piece of wedding cake!

"Zalman!" I yelled at the sneak-cheat friend high in the branches above. "Zalman! You stinker! That's a rotten trick to play, hiding from me like that!"

"Ha! Ha! I scared you!" he shouted with a laugh. "I scared you—ooooh! You should have seen your face!"

He leaned his head back and laughed like an imp. His deep-brown eyes were lit with laughter, and his black curly earlocks stuck out from his head like little bedsprings. The more he laughed, the angrier I got; so when he climbed to a lower branch and jumped to the ground, I gave him some good punches.

"You sneak!" I shouted.

"You baby!" he taunted, punching me back. "You jumped! You really did jump!" And he laughed even harder as he made quick, startled jumps.

"That's what you did," he yelled, "just like that! . . ."

"I didn't!" I shouted back, socking him in the shoulder.

"You did!"

"I didn't!"

"You did! You almost jumped out of your skin!"

I was winding up to give him another punch when he suddenly shouted, "Wait! Wait! I almost forgot!"

I stepped back, and he ran to the pine tree and climbed back up. "What's up there?" I shouted.

"It's a surprise!" he shouted back.

From a small hole in the trunk he took out a tiny parcel wrapped in a rag. He climbed down very carefully. "Wait till you see the one I made this time," he said. "It's the most beautiful of all."

At once I forgot how I'd been tricked. I simply stared at the mysterious package.

"Just look!" Zalman whispered as he unfolded the dirty rag to reveal a delicate wooden boat.

"Can I hold it?" I asked.

"Sure."

I held the toy, cradling it gently in both hands. It was a tiny vessel carved from soft pinewood. It had two topsails and a mainsail neatly glued to slender twig masts, further secured by inch-long stretches of old violin string. The deck rails were fashioned from skinny pine strips that had been soaked and then curved around the deck of the ship. The miniature sails were of thin cotton and snowy white.

"Your papa's handkerchief?"

"And who else's?" Zalman replied.

"Won't he be angry?"

"*Ach!* He'll never miss it. Who blows his nose in springtime? Let's sail it!"

"Of course," I agreed. And then, because somehow whenever Zalman and I did something together I always ended up in trouble, I warned, "But we can't go in with it or we'll get our clothes wet, and Cabbage Ears Svinsky will crack our heads. Better to use a string and lead it from the shore."

As I spoke, Zalman pulled a dirty piece of string from his pocket. He tied one end to the small hole in the bow. Then we placed the boat in the quick green waters of the Dniester. "Come on, let's race it," Zalman said. We took turns holding the string as we walked along the riverbank, steering the boat up and over the treacherous pebbles.

The boat bobbed up and down. The wind ballooned the thin sails out and slapped them quickly against the thin masts. It sailed faster and faster. I loved the little boat. It was no bigger than a *Shabbos* candle, yet it seemed to me no longer a toy but a small ship on a very large sea. All my longing to travel and to know about things outside our village was caught up in watching that boat. I felt suddenly buoyant too, unfettered, happy. "Isn't she beautiful?" I cried aloud.

"Of course," Zalman called, "and look how she handles herself!" He was walking backward, quickly pulling the boat, and he didn't see the narrow ditch in back of him.

"Look out!" I yelled.

"Look out for what?" he shouted back.

"Look out for the . . ."

Too late. Zalman tumbled backward. The string snapped in his hand, and the little boat tipped over.

I leapt on a rock and stretched my arm out as far as I could, to grab it, but the rock was slippery and I fell, cutting my knee and soaking my breeches. The boat lodged between two rocks—smashed. I picked it out of the water. "One of the masts is broken," I called, "and there's a hole in the side!"

Climbing out of the ditch, breeches and jacket painted with mud, Zalman inspected the toy closely.

"It's not so bad," he said. "Could be worse. Look, the hole is small, and I can fix the mast."

We walked back to the pine tree. Zalman wrapped the pieces of toy in the rag, climbed up the tree, and stuffed the parcel deep within the trunk hollow. "We'll leave it here until I have time to work on it," he said. I agreed this was safer than bringing it home. Zalman's father and sisters didn't understand his love for carving, and his mother probably would have used it for kindling. "We'll sail it soon," Zalman said, not seeming at all troubled by the boat's damage. "And who knows? Maybe we'll have a passenger next time. There's a mouse in our woodpile who'd make a good sailor. But don't tell anyone about the boat, all right?"

"So who would I tell?"

"I don't know. I just don't want all the first-year students or Dovid to find out about it ... do you?" Zalman's face was serious.

"Of course not," I answered. "I won't tell anyone."

"Swear it then," said Zalman.

"I will not tell a living person about this boat," I swore, holding the fringes of my prayer shawl. "And if I do, may the Evil Eye plant onions in my navel."

Just as I finished my oath, the Sunday ringing of church bells broke the quiet of the riverbank. Soon the Christian peasants would be gathering for Mass while we—who observed the Sabbath on Saturday—would be studying the *Torah* under the watchful eye of Reb Svinsky.

"Come," I yelled, "we'll be late for school!"

"Oy!" wailed Zalman, "I don't want to feel Cabbage Ears's *khantchik!*"

Running like demons up the path, we dashed through the streets, being especially careful to run far around the churchgoers. Moments before we reached Reb Svinsky's hut a flock of swallows flew overhead.

"Bom Tshi-tshe! Bom Tshi-tshe!" we yelled up to them. "Give me a piece of wedding cake!" Then putting on our God–fearing faces, we opened the schoolroom door.

3

"Not Dovid . . . not Chaim . . . not Yossie . . . not Yankel . . ." Reb Svinsky was taking the roll and at the same time fooling the Evil Eye. What bad spirit could do harm to children who were not there? "Not Kalmen . . . not Asher . . . not Itzhak . . ."

When he got to "not Itzhak," he turned from the class to stare at us in the doorway. For several moments he just glared at us in growing anger, then he started toward us, shouting. "Torah students who wallow in the mud!" *CRACK!* The khantchik, Reb Svinsky's little whip, crashed down on my knuckles. *CRACK!* The khantchik crashed down on Zalman's.

I let out a cry and my eyes stung with tears, but Zalman made not a sound. Out of the corner of my eye I could see Dovid's smirking face. Reb Svinsky shut the door behind us and pushed us inside. "Sit in your filth all day, and let it be a sign of your disgrace!" Reb Svinsky said.

CRACK! Another strike of the khantchik broke sharply on our outstretched fingers.

"Sit down. Sit down. We'll see if you know your lessons . . . and you other fools, pipe down or you'll get the same!" As Zalman and I moved to our seats, I saw all the whispering boys on the benches suddenly trying to look pious.

We were fourteen boys crowded together in a shabby hut. The six- and seven-year-olds squeezed up front, and we older boys studying *Talmud*—Dovid, Chaim, Yossie, Zalman, and I—huddled on the splintery benches in the back.

We were a funny looking group. The younger boys seemed to wear clothes too large, and the older ones, clothes too small. The little ones wore hand-me-downs: someone else's shoes, baggy breeches, shirts with the sleeves hemmed up to the elbows. In winter their knit hats slid down over their eyes, and their runny noses got wiped on the sagging sleeves of discarded coats. The older boys, including myself, wore broken shoes, while the jackets straining at the buttons, the breeches splitting at the seams, and the grayed wool scarves wrapping our necks made us look as if we would at any moment burst from our clothes—like butterflies from drab cocoons.

"Mendel Cholinsky, you first today." At Reb Svinsky's command I opened my book and began. As I read, I rocked gently back and forth to keep the rhythm of the Hebrew words.

"It is not the place that honors the man but the man that honors the . . . the pace . . . I mean . . . not the pace . . . the . . . *place*." Reb Svinsky looked at me menacingly and I continued, "Do not consider yourself a giant and your neighbor small as a locust. Let a man be yielding as a reed in the wind, not hard and unbending like cedar."

"Not so bad," Reb Svinsky said. "It's a wonder, Mendel, what a few smacks can do." He turned to Zalman and yanked his earlock. "Now you, troublemaker."

Zalman stood and began to read, swaying like a young branch in the wind. He read in a loud, clear voice of measured passion, and even the first-year boys stopped playing with their fingers and listened.

These are the things which the Lord hateth,
*   which are an abomination unto Him.*
Haughty eyes, a lying tongue,
*   and hands that shed innocent blood.*
A heart that devises wicked, evil thoughts.
Feet that are swift to do evil.
Envy not the man of violence and choose none of his ways.

"Not so bad," Reb Svinsky nodded, "not so bad. But you could do even better, yes, even better. Now Yossie, let us see if a lamb like you can bleat these lines . . . yes?"

Our lesson went on for hours. In the mornings we stood reading together, bowing and swaying in unison, so that the motion of all the boys made the room seem to bob as a boat on the river. In the afternoons we had to sit and read silently to ourselves, and to me this was the hardest. Though it was early spring, it was cold in the room. The law forbade Jews from traveling, even to gather firewood in Pinski forest. The price of coal had risen too high for Reb Svinsky to afford; so as I read, I shivered.

I strained at the boxy black letters before me, but I couldn't concentrate. When I saw the rounded letter *samech*, ▢, I saw a bagel, hot and spread with herring. When I saw the letter *vav*, ⅂, I saw a beef sausage, fat and juicy. My stomach grumbled. My mind wandered. From outside I heard the song of birds, and I yearned to be with all things that were free.

As he read, Reb Svinsky stroked his beard. He was deep in thought. I tore a scrap of paper from my notebook and wrote:

> *The teacher we call Cabbage Ears*
> *Whips the boys and brings them tears*
> *But I would rather sail a boat*
> *Than be whipped by that old goat!*

I folded the paper, coughed three times, my secret signal to Zalman, and stretched out my arm to pass it to him. Zalman reached for it, but not far enough. I stretched even further and so did Zalman, but he still couldn't grab it. I leaned just a bit farther until with a terrible noise, I fell to the floor.

Reb Svinsky sprang up. "What craziness is this?" he yelled. "Get up!" I tried to untangle my legs and at the same time kick the paper clear under the bench where he might not see it. "Get up, foolish boy! Get up!" he commanded, charging at me. I struggled to my feet. "What were you doing on the floor?"

"Nothing, Reb . . . I just fell."

"Come, tell the truth! Now!"

"I was studying very, very hard, Reb Svinsky . . . so hard I lost my balance."

"What do you mean?" he asked, glaring down at me.

"I . . . I was thrown off balance by . . . by the weight of the great words in the Torah."

"I see," he said sarcastically. I tried to look up at him bravely, but right behind him I could see Dovid quietly pushing the paper with his foot. Pushing it out from under the bench—directly into Reb Svinsky's view!

Paralyzed with fear, I said nothing. "But what is *this*?" Our teacher picked up the scrap and silently read my poem. I felt my face grow hot. "Is this your handiwork?" he asked me.

"No," I said. "I mean, I don't think so."

Reb Svinsky wheeled around to face Zalman and thundered, "Is it yours?"

Zalman coughed.

"Well . . . is it?"

"It could be," Zalman muttered.

"No, it's not his," I said, and before I could confess Dovid said, "It's Mendel's, Reb Svinsky, I saw him writing it just a minute ago."

As punishment I got eight whips of the khantchik. But I hardly felt the pain, for I was plotting my revenge against Dovid. He was much bigger than I was and far more brave, but somehow I'd batter him.

4

By the time school was over, night had come. Each student lit his candle and headed for home. Dovid, who had no friends, hung back, slowly kicking up dirt as he walked. "Dovid, I'm going to batter you!" I shouted recklessly. The words were out. There was no turning back.

"Are you crazy?" Zalman cried. "The Rag Rat will slaughter you!"

"I'm not afraid," I said, even though my heart was beating like a bird's.

Dovid blew out his candle and walked toward me slowly. His thin jacket had long since lost its buttons, and his arms, long and powerful, hung below his scanty sleeves. My knees felt weak, and I thought my head would burst. "Run!" Zalman yelled, "RUN!" But I stood fixed—less from courage than from fear. I handed Zalman my candle. Dovid stuck his bruised, hard face inches away from my own. "What do *you* want, *K'vatsh*?"

He alone called me K'vatsh, which was our Yiddish word for coward. He stared at me in anger. His hair was dark and greasy, as if painted on, and his teeth were crooked. I could feel his warm, sour breath. I wanted to answer. I wanted to say, "I'm going to beat you up, you rotten son of a ragpicker!" But suddenly I was too afraid to say anything.

"K'VATSH!" he shouted in my face, and that's when I kicked him hard in the leg. He flinched for a second, and the next thing I saw was his fist moving toward my head. I stumbled back from the blow, and he punched me in the stomach. Then I was lying on the dirt street, my head on fire. The wind was knocked out of me. I couldn't talk, only gasp. As if in a dream I heard Dovid's words as he stood over me. "See? I can beat you up quick and easy. Remember that, K'VATSH!"

I must have lain there for some time. At last I slowly lifted myself up. My mouth filled with a warm liquid, and I felt hands on my shoulders. "Get up! Get up! Please, Mendel, get up!" Zalman was pulling on me. I thought my head would explode. He held the candle close to my head. From the expression on Zalman's face, I knew what my own looked like. I stumbled to my feet groggily. The streets were deserted now.

Zalman held my arm, and we stumbled down the street together. "Dovid pounded me," I groaned.

"That's because Rag Rat's *bigger* than you," Zalman

said, "that's all." But I knew the truth. I knew that for all my brave words, I didn't really want to fight Dovid . . . I was afraid of him. Dovid was braver than I was. Meaner—but braver.

We crossed through the dark alleys. The little shops were closed and unlit. Everything was black and strangely quiet. "Where are all the Jews tonight?" Zalman asked nervously. "Where's Old Hershel the *droshky* driver? Where's Meyer with his water buckets? Where are the men walking home from evening prayers?"

"I don't know," I answered, spitting the blood from my mouth.

We felt exposed and alone in this unnatural quiet. We walked past the marketplace, then split up. Zalman took the narrow road to the left, and I went along the dirt road that stretched up the hill. The Jewish graveyard next to our hut at the top of the hill never bothered me during the day. But now, as I looked up, I could see the outlines of tombs rising like ghosts in the moonlight. I began to run, and my candle went out. In the blackness I prayed continuously, so no tombstone spirit could grab me. And as I ran, praying, the sound of my footsteps seemed to echo, "K'vatsh, K'vatsh, K'vatsh, K'vatsh."

5

My head throbbing with pain and my stomach grumbling for food, I threaded my way past the bean vines in front of our hut. I pushed the splintery wooden door. But it wouldn't open! I pushed again, then banged on the door with my fist. The door opened suddenly, and my mother came out and shut it behind her.

"Thank the Lord, you're here!" she exclaimed. "I've been worried sick. Why must you dawdle? Were you playing the fool with that imp, Zalman? Oy! And what happened to your head?!" Her eyes filled with fear. "Who did this to you?" she cried.

"I was in a fight with Dovid, Mama."

"Fight! It is wrong to fight!" she wailed. The air was cold, and I started to shiver, but she yanked me over to the pump and washed my face and hands as if I were a baby. "I'll get you a rag for your head. But look at your clothes, dirty and torn!" Mama opened the door and pushed me inside. "Now sit. Sit anywhere!"

She made a sweeping gesture toward the villagers gathered in our hut. I stared stupidly at the crowd. Never had I seen so many people in my home. On the floor sat Papa, and beside him the Litsky brothers, Solomon One-Eye, and Meyer the Water Carrier. Avraham the Baker and Zenvil the Knife Sharpener were squeezed into the corner by the stove. On the opposite side of the tiny room sat the women, some still wearing their soiled aprons. My aunt Zifra sat on a cushion on the floor. Meyer's wife, Dora Ruthka, Avraham's fat wife, Gittel, and my mother were curled up together on the bed. Three babies of different sizes gurgled happily alongside.

I sat on the floor next to Aunt Zifra. My mind was spinning like a *dreidel*. Why were all these people here in my home . . . and at suppertime?

"The dark streets are no place for a boy!" Aunt Zifra whispered in my ear, giving me a stern look but pressing my cold hand warmly in her own.

Mama brought me cabbage soup and a slice of bread. "Eat quietly and don't make any bother tonight," she whispered. "Hershel's been killed."

"Old Hershel! Why? Why would anyone kill a droshky driver?"

"Don't ask. Only God knows such things!"

"Who did it?"

"Peasants—several of them." Mama answered impatiently. "*Shaa!* Don't talk or Papa will get angry."

Dora Ruthka was speaking to the other grown-ups. Her knitting needles clucked like chickens as she spoke her mind. "If things don't get better, depend on it, they will get worse! Today the peasants killed Hershel, tomorrow, who will it be? The violence against us will not stop. The peasants hate us. They are angry. They are tired of being slaves to the landowners; yet they take their hatred out on us!"

"Why us?" Solomon One-Eye asked angrily. "Is it our fault they are poor? We are just as poor!" Solomon beamed his eye on the group and shouted, "But it *is* the fault of the czar! It is the czar himself who allows the rich landowners to treat the peasants like slaves; yet it is the czar who tells the peasants *we* are wicked. It is he who is wicked! His Majesty, Czar Nicholas!"

"You are right, Solomon," Avraham the Baker said excitedly. "This 'Iron Czar' has made hundreds of laws against us. We cannot own land. We cannot travel freely from one town to another. We cannot bake *matzos* or gather wood. We are fined when we do not dress as the peasants do and fined when we print our Hebrew books. We cannot go to university or learn a trade. We are helpless; yet while we live, we dare not speak."

"And when we are dead, we cannot," Aunt Zifra added with a sigh.

"Excuse me," Meyer the Water Carrier said. "I am

not an educated man. You can't learn much from the daily babbling of a river. But if you send your ears into the street, you will hear that fighters for freedom, the Idealists perhaps, will rise up against this czar. The hatred and violence will stop. All change will come, but it will take time . . . we cannot expect spring to follow autumn."

"Fighters for freedom!" Avraham hooted. "With their high-and-mighty talk of justice, most of these 'freedom fighters' are also against us!"

"And how do you know?" Meyer asked.

"I know because I read Russian."

Many of us could speak Russian, but Avraham was the only one among us who could read it. He fumbled in his tattered coat and brought out a crumpled pamphlet. Squinting hard at the paper, he mumbled the Russian words under his breath and then spoke them aloud to us in Yiddish.

GOOD PEOPLE! HONEST UKRAINIAN PEOPLE! THE LANDOWNERS OWN YOU, BUT THE DIRTY JEWS ROB YOU. WHO HAS SEIZED THE SHOPS AND THE TAVERNS? THE JEWS! WHEREVER YOU LOOK, WHATEVER YOU TOUCH, THE JEWS. THE JEW CURSES THE PEASANT, CHEATS HIM, DRINKS HIS BLOOD. ARISE! WREAK YOUR VENGEANCE ON THE LANDOWNERS, KILL THE OFFICIALS, BUT ALSO KILL THE JEWS!

Avraham crumpled the pamphlet into a ball and threw it onto our dirt floor. "These are your freedom fighters!"

"May they choke on their words!" his wife Gittel cursed.

Zenvil the Knife Sharpener stroked his brown beard. "If we want to stop our own destruction," he said, "we have two choices: fight or flee."

My father, who all this while had been silent, now spoke. "We can pray," he said. "Prayer has always been our way. We have faith that God will provide."

"But who will provide," Zenvil asked, "*until* He provides?"

The room was silent—perhaps because we all saw the truth in Zenvil's words. Our life was as tenuous as the spring snow on our roofs. I looked at the faces of the villagers as the fire crackled; and the soot that always condensed on our ceiling when the stove was burning, dripped now and then to the floor in black gritty drops, every so often dropping on someone silently. I felt a sudden pity for all of us. I had often heard my mother call us *luftmenshen*, air people, for we lived on things you couldn't hold or see. On dreams and prayers. Our work was real, but only within this little town in which we were forced to live. We had to survive by trading with each other. Beyond Molovsk we could not travel, let alone seek education or jobs. We could not own land in Molovsk; yet it was our home. Sometimes it seemed to me that, beyond Molovsk, we would all float away, like seeds of a dandelion in a strong wind.

"I heard something terrible at the market," Dora Ruthka announced suddenly. We all looked at her pained face. "People are saying the czar is going to increase Jewish military conscription. They say war will break out soon against England, and more soldiers are needed than ever before. Czar Nicholas wants more children now too. Even Jewish boys as young as twelve will be forced to join the czar's army!"

"No!" my mother said, firmly dismissing the idea. "Certainly the czar would not urge such a foolish thing . . . what good are a lot of Jewish children to him? Besides, the officials in Kiev will have better sense than to allow such madness here."

Dora Ruthka looked hard at my mother and said, "Pesha, for years Jewish children have been torn from their families and put into the Cantonist brigades. Just because conscription hasn't happened in Molovsk yet, doesn't mean it can't."

Zenvil removed his left boot and unlatched the small leather sheath hidden in its lining. He drew out a narrow, sharp knife and held it horizontally in front of him. "Our road through life is like the edge of a blade, with the netherworld on either side. Those of us who do not die of starvation will die of violence."

"Zenvil," my mother said softly, "what do you suggest we do?"

Zenvil carefully fitted the knife back into the sheath, then looked up at her. "Leave Russia."

Dora Ruthka put down her needles and nodded. "In

Germany a Jew is a person. He is left alone, and no one hurts him. He can be an officer in the army, go to medical school, even teach in the university!"

"Excuse me," Zenvil interrupted, "but it is not of Germany I am talking. I am talking about the place where we can start over, forge a new life in a new country. I am speaking to you now of America. In America the law is the same for Jew as for gentile. In America a shoemaker is as free as a king."

I glanced at my father's thin, bearded face. His large dark eyes were thoughtful. I knew what was coming.

"Don't talk of America," Papa said gravely. "What is this freedom you speak of? Freedom to cut our beards? Freedom to eat pork? Freedom to work on the Shabbos?"

"Papa," I said, surprising myself with my boldness. "In America there is freedom to *learn* things."

My father stared at me in disbelief, yet he said calmly, "My son, you are a child and do not know what you say. America is not for Jews. Even the foolish attempt to *get* to America has claimed many Jewish lives."

"Yes, the Green Border is dangerous," Solomon One-Eye said, his face sad and incomplete. "Very few succeed in escaping, but is it better to be killed here in captivity—like Hershel . . . or to die on the way to freedom?"

Nobody spoke. We all knew the answer. The Green Border was the way of the brave. From our Ukrainian province it was the frontier of thick forests that separated Russia from the Austrian Empire—the illegal border of dense bushes and night shadows, hidden from guards. From farm to farm, and wood to wood, crossing the Green Border was a dangerous course, most often ending in capture and death.

Gittel spoke up. Her plump face was red with excitement. "I believe many Jews have been aided by the man some call Valdi who, they say, helps people steal across the border. I've heard whisperings that a small group of Idealists are helping anyone—even Jews—escape Russia. They say this Valdi, who is one of them, is trustworthy. They say he can be found in many places, and often at the new station at Pereginsko. They say he . . ."

"Russia is our home," Papa interrupted. "God Himself placed us here!"

My mother played with the stray locks that peeked out from under her babushka. She looked thoughtful. Perhaps she was thinking of her older sister, my aunt Bella, who had gone to America with her husband five years ago. Aunt Bella had written letters of the wonders of New York. Now my mother said soothingly, "Each of us must find the answer. Solomon, if you or anyone else in this room wants to leave, we can only pray for you. For us," Mama said with finality, "it is not the way."

The grown-up talk went on and on; and when they all left, I washed the rest of the dirt off me, then went to bed. My mother sat by the flickering oil lantern, sewing—making me a new jacket from Avraham's old coat. My father sat alongside her, reading from his prayer book. As I lay in bed I thought of what Dora Ruthka had said: "Even Jewish boys as young as twelve will be forced to join the czar's army." I was twelve, but I knew I wasn't a man yet. Didn't you have to be a man to be a soldier? I wondered about this for a long time as the soot drops plonked to the earth floor.

6

"So your parents let you come today?" Zalman asked, skipping another stone into the river.

"No," I answered, "I told them I was going to study with Chaim."

"Oy! Not Chaim Head-Nodder? Picking up corn and chicken fodder!"

Zalman stuck his elbows out to make chicken wings and clucked and pecked around in a circle, exaggerating our classmate's habit of bobbing his head up and down as he talked.

We both collapsed on the ground laughing. Zalman stuffed his *yarmulke* in his bulging pocket and did two handsprings. Wednesdays we only went to school in the morning, and so now on this afternoon, we were savoring the special stolen time. I lifted the mended boat high into the air. "Let's see how she sails!" I cried.

We ran toward the sun-sparkled water of the river

and floated the toy. It sailed even better than before. Its slim body rode the waves gracefully, and the tall sails, now attached to thicker twigs, were perfectly balanced.

"Wouldn't you like to sail on a boat like that?" Zalman asked me as I pulled it along with the string. "A real boat?"

It was my dearest wish; yet I answered, "Jews don't go sailing."

"Sure they do!" Zalman cried. "Don't you remember what the Torah says: 'And King Solomon made a navy of ships in Ezion-geber.' That navy sailed to Ophir and found gold there, lots of it, and brought it back to King Solomon."

"That was a long time ago," I answered. "Jews have no ships of their own now. Only the Jews who make it across the Green Border can sail on ships. From Germany to America."

"I'll do that," Zalman said matter-of-factly. "My parents talk of leaving. They say it is too dangerous here. They say that all the boys will soon have to join the Cantonist brigades!"

"*My* parents say it is just talk," I said.

"If it's 'just talk' why did Zenvil hear in the marketplace yesterday that officers from Kiev may be coming to take a survey of all Jewish families in Molovsk?"

My heart froze at this news; yet I answered, "Just talk."

"Well, *I* believe it," Zalman said and then mused, "but I don't think I'd be afraid if they did. I don't want to go to the army, but I'd be as brave as anyone. I'd be a good soldier, maybe become a famous general!"

I looked at Zalman, shocked. "You're crazy! A Jew can never be an officer. Never! You wouldn't get a chance to be famous."

"Well, I'd be brave anyway," he boasted.

"Brave? You'd have to be brave! Dora Ruthka said Jews are taken far away from the Pale for twenty-five years and all that time can never return to see their families. Not even once."

For a while neither he nor I said a word. Then he began fishing in his pocket for something.

"What are you looking for?"

"You'll see . . . something special."

Failing in his search, Zalman turned his pockets inside out, and at once wood shavings, bread crusts, tiny balls of string, twigs, pinecones, pebbles, and something long and black fell out. Zalman picked up this mysterious object and handed it to me while he stuffed the other things back in his pocket.

I opened the top of a ragged leather case and drew out a silver knife. The heavy handle was carved with a lion's head. Though dented in two places, the blade was shiny and sharp.

"It was my great-grandfather's," Zalman explained. "He gave it to my grandfather who gave it to my father, and now my father gave it to me. See, he's already had it inscribed for me."

I flipped the knife over and saw "Zalman" written in

ornate Hebrew letters on the other side of the blade.

"If I ever cross the Green Border, this will come in handy," Zalman said. "I could skin small animals, carve a fishing pole, or fight off a snake!"

"It's beautiful," I said.

"It's the most beautiful thing I own," he declared solemnly, as he slipped the knife back into its tattered case and slid it into his pocket. "It's so precious that I've already picked out a secret hiding place for it—under the roof thatch over our window."

"Zalman, do you really think you will cross the Green Border?"

"Why not? My father says Jews are hated in Russia, and so there is no choice but escape. He says we must be prepared to escape at any time. Maybe your parents will leave too. Maybe one day we'll meet in America!"

"I don't think so," I said. "My mother and father think differently. They say God gives us courage to stay and be strong, not to run away like mice."

We had followed the riverbank almost as far as the church. When we realized where we were, Zalman pulled in the boat and we turned back. At the pine tree again, we wrapped the boat and put it back in the trunk hollow. Then we lay on our stomachs and lazily watched the river. For a long while neither of us said a word. The air smelled sweetly green, and the water flowed swiftly, making the sound of crumpling paper. In the distance a barge, piled high with logs, floated southward. Where it was going I didn't know, but the swift current of the river and its constant journey made me feel all the more restless. I knew that, like all rivers, the Dniester held the heartbeat of the sea, and this thought stirred me with an unbearable longing to leave. To sail away. To go.

I closed my eyes and prayed my parents would change their minds.

7

When the spring peddlers came through Molovsk, they brought news of terrible things they'd seen in the eastern provinces. The peddlers told how more than 30,000 children had been conscripted there already. The czar, they said, was now giving rewards to the officers who recruited the most children. They described the pitiful sights they'd seen: crying children yanked away from their mothers and public whippings of parents who protested. The ribbon peddler told the worst story of all. "I was traveling through a small town far to the east of Polotsk," he said, "when I saw a young boy, perhaps thirteen, being marched through the streets by soldiers. The boy's left foot was wrapped crudely in a dirty shirt, and he dragged it piteously along as if it were a stone. As he went, a great crowd of people stood weeping; yet all were too terrified to cry out, all except his mother, whose wailing was so loud that heaven's angels could have heard her without straining. 'Who is that luckless child?' I asked an old man in the crowd. The old man, his eyes wet with tears told me that on seeing soldiers approach his home, this boy took an axe and cut off three toes of his left foot so as not to be conscripted. But the czar's soldiers are heartless men, and they took him anyway."

We listened in horror to the peddlers, and then sometime in late June a rumor went around Molovsk that treasury officials from Kiev would be coming to take children. Behind our wood shutters and window rags we lived in terror. How much longer, we thought, can tiny Molovsk remain untouched by the czar's madness? But the weeks went by, and with their peaceful passing our worries gradually subsided.

In July my father went, as every year, to Count Oroskoff's estate to renew his permit to travel between the villages. Each year my father gave the count sixty *rubles*: thirty for the permit and thirty for the rental of a cart and the old horse, Taki. It was an exorbitant price to pay, especially because everything Papa transported belonged to the count anyway. Papa was paid by the overseers on the local farms, which were owned by the count and really were part of his estate. Mama often said, "The count is charging us a fortune so we can carry and sell *his* produce!" But what else could we do? It was the only way my father had to make any money. From sunup to sundown he transported potatoes to Volmynsk and loaded the heavy bags of oats, rye, and wheat from the farms around Molovsk and those of Rinnitsa. In late August, even during the summer storms, bales of plums had to be taken to distant Kerdichev. And though the count forbade it, all summer the poorest peasants and Jews would barter to ride in the cart, three *kopeks* from Molovsk to Starokonstantinov and four kopeks to Kholov.

The day Papa went to the count was Friday. Mama and I were preparing for Shabbos. She was cutting noodle dough, spreading it out like a cloth on our table. I was outside trying to chop wood. I was not good at it. My strokes were feeble, and often I missed the block altogether. My shoulders ached, and too many times I got the axe stuck in the wood and was forced to pry it out with both hands and my foot too. It was at times like this that I wondered why God couldn't have made me big like Dovid.

When I finally chopped all the wood, I built the logs into a pile and stuck the axe into the block. That was the last of the firewood. From now on we'd have to buy turf from the peasants or ask permission to collect dung from the count's cow pastures. I washed my hands at the pump and went inside. I swept the flax mats, and as I worked beside my mother, I thought how different things were now.

Shabbos had always been a time of quiet, but lately it held the quiet of unspoken worry. I knew my parents worried about money, and they worried about the army conscription. I knew that late at night when they thought

I was asleep, they talked in troubled voices to each other.

That day, as my mother and I worked in silence, I thought about my father. "Mama," I asked, "do you think Papa will get the travel permit and the cart again this year?"

"If God wills it," Mama answered.

"If God wills it, Mama, will Papa let me ride with him to Kholov or Kerdichev?" I loved going with my father, not only because I loved the time with him, but if I pleaded, my father often unhitched the cart and let me ride, even gallop sometimes, on Taki's back. I had become good at it.

"You will do more than just ride with your father, Mendel," Mama answered. "This year you will help your father in his work."

"How can I help him?"

"He will teach you how to drive the wagon. This is an important thing to know."

I put my broom down. "Drive a wagon myself?" I couldn't believe what my mother had just said. She had always tried to protect me from the world, but now she was talking as if she wanted me to be a grown-up.

"But Mama, you are always saying I am too young for such things!"

My mother walked to the stove, handed me the black pot and said, "There comes a time, Mendel, when what you are, and what you will be, meet. Now take the stew and come back quickly."

I took the pot and headed for the door, but when I

got there I turned and asked, "Will you or Papa tell me when that time comes?"

"No, Mendel," she said. "No one will tell you. But you will know."

Holding the pot with both hands, I headed for Avraham and Gittel's bakery. When I reached Volminsky Street, I darted quickly through the noisy throngs of people. A group of Jewish men in long black coats and wide fur hats passed me, heading toward the ritual bathhouse. Not far behind, soldiers with gleaming swords and buttons that glittered like gold coins laughed about something and stopped to talk to a peasant. It was rare to see this many soldiers about; and remembering what my mother said, I did not dawdle, for today the streets held the tension of Jews and gentiles mingling. I jumped quickly over every crack on Volminsky Street without bumping into anyone. I reached the tiny bakery and placed our stew on the counter.

"So, Mendel, how is your family getting on?" Gittel's stout face looked kindly down at me.

"Fine, thank you," I replied. Gittel took the pot, and I hoped she would not peek inside and see our stew had no meat. She did not look at it but simply labeled the pot and slid it into her oven. While she did this, I stared at the hot apple turnovers cooling on the wood boards and breathed in their warm, sweet smell. Next to the riverbank, I loved the bakery better than any place in Molovsk. During the week it sent out the fragrance of sweet jam rolls, cinnamon cakes, honey cakes, and apple tarts. Now on Shabbos Eve it had the added steamy aroma of the stews the Jewish families brought to cook in the huge bakery oven. It was forbidden to light a fire on Shabbos, and our stews took a long time to cook. But this way they would cook slowly on the hot coals all night and be collected the next evening after Shabbos ended.

Gittel turned back to me and peered into my face. "So what do you say, Mendel, will your papa be going for the permit again this year?"

"Yes, ma'am, he went to see the count this morning."

"This morning already? I hope he gets it, but I heard the count is reluctant now to help Jews in any way."

"Yes, but he had promised my father the permit again for this year."

"Oy! Count Oroskoff promised! Pardon me for saying this, but what can his promises mean? If the count's words were a bridge, I wouldn't cross it!"

"Yes, ma'am."

Gittel stared at me and I felt embarrassed. She looked hard at my worn jacket, my rag-stuffed shoes, and my skinny legs. She unfolded a sheet of newspaper, and her dry, plump hands carefully wrapped three apple turnovers into a neat package.

"You won't drop it now, will you Mendel?"

I took the package, searching for the right words to thank her, but all I heard myself say was, "Three apple turnovers!"

"Yes," she said, "that's what they are, and enjoy them. Have a sweet Shabbos, and Mendel . . ."

I turned and saw a troubled look on her face.

"Don't stay in town too long. You know that soldiers from Kiev arrived this morning, and now the streets crawl with them."

"Why are they here?" I asked.

"I wish I knew, Mendel. I wish I knew!"

Out in the street I blended into the small crowds of people bustling from shop to shop. Shabbos Eve was always a busy time. Since the shops closed early, people had to rush to get what they needed. Housewives wrapped in shawls weaved in and out of the shops of the slaughterer, the fishmonger, the baker, and through the vegetable and spice sellers' stands that crowded the streets. Zenvil sat at his wheel, sharpening knives, scissors, and axes. Though market day was Wednesday, several peasants brought their produce in on Friday to sell to the Jewish housewives. A young man sold beets right out of his wheelbarrow, while two old women sat by a box of carrots in a shop doorway.

I went quickly, holding the turnover parcel tightly. Though I was tempted to see if I could endure hopping all the way down Volminsky Street, and though I longed to run to the Dniester and throw rocks into its deep water, I headed straight for home. But as I went, the sound of shouting stopped me in my tracks.

"Three kopeks is the price—I said it plainly!"

"I will give you one kopek and not a kopek more!"

"You cannot get six knives sharpened for one kopek! You owe me two more kopeks!"

I looked to see where these angry words came from. Zenvil was arguing with one of the peasants who worked on Count Oroskoff's estate. Now a crowd was forming around them.

"I owe you nothing!"

"You owe me two kopeks!"

"Go to hell, you dirty Jew!"

In reply, Zenvil lifted a knife in the air in a threatening manner. I wanted to scream, "DON'T!" but just then four soldiers ran up, seized Zenvil, and began beating him. The crowd started to shout, push, and shove. A Jew and a peasant began a fistfight. Then two young women started shoving each other. I saw soldiers down the street running toward the brawl, and that's when I started to run away from it. I ran down Koolof Street, but before I had gotten very far someone pushed me hard from behind. Deliberately. I stumbled forward, and my package flew out of my hands, soaring like a bird ahead of me. It was then I saw a tall boy run from behind me, swoop down, and catch the package in midair. He held it tight against his chest; and when he turned to grin at me, I saw the cruel face of Dovid.

8

I ran all the way home, and by the time I got there my father was just arriving, riding high up on the cart. In the excitement of seeing my father returning from Count Oroskoff, I buried the news of the street fight and the stolen turnovers.

Mama ran outside to greet him, wearing her blue Shabbos dress. My father sat up on the driver's ledge, silent. I could see Mama sensed something amiss, for she asked softly, "Naftali, the count agreed to lend you the permit, yes?"

Papa climbed down from the wagon but did not answer. My mother repeated her question.

"No," my father said gruffly. "We cannot have the permit this year. No Jew can travel between the villages."

"But he's let you keep the cart!" my mother exclaimed.

"Yes, I have the cart today, but I cannot have it this year. Count Oroskoff wants me to make my last delivery from Smalnysk on Wednesday, and then return the cart and the horse to him. The count said, 'Now and forever, the generosity we have shown the Jews is over, and I will make no exception for you, Naftali!' "

"But, my husband, the use of the horse and cart was *promised* to us! I don't mean to criticize you, but could you not have pleaded with him a little?"

"Don't be foolish!" Papa snapped. "What could I have said to him?" He climbed down from the cart and looked at Mama's anguished face. "Pesha," he said softly, "I had no choice, and no choice *is* a choice."

I could tell from her face that Mama wanted to say something more. And I knew what it was, for I was thinking the same thing. She wanted to say that now we had nothing to live on but the coins from the rags she could sell or the clothes she could wash. She wanted to say that now we would not be able to afford fish or shoes or jam, and maybe not even flour. She wanted to say many things, but seeing my father's face, she said nothing.

"We will talk about it later," Papa said wearily, "not on Shabbos."

While my father washed up, I unharnessed Taki, brushed her carefully, and fed her. Then I washed also, and went inside.

Our hut smelled of the fish Mama had simmered just before sundown. She had long since sold our little silver candlesticks, so now she stuck each Shabbos candle into a ball of leftover noodle dough. Mama lit the candles—our only fire allowed on Shabbos—and with her eyes shut, whispered the prayers. She welcomed the Sabbath into our home. Then she moved her arms slowly over the candles to hug the holiness that rose from the flames. After prayers my mother brought in our meal. In the twilight we ate the peppered carp, the noodles, and bread. We ate in silence, and my heart was heavy. The small carp was barely enough for the three of us, and I thought how much nicer the meal would have been with the apple turnovers. But then my thoughts turned to Zenvil, and I worried that he was hurt badly. I was also nervous at the number of soldiers on the streets. But I said nothing of my thoughts. And my mother mentioned not a word about the permit. Whatever happened in the world was not for us to speak of. Not on Shabbos.

After supper, when Mama nestled in bed to read her Yiddish prayer book, Papa and I stayed at the table, and like every Friday night, we talked. This was the time I loved best of all. The rest of the week my father spoke to me sternly, but on Shabbos his manner toward me was warm, and his thoughts were as bright as if the Shabbos lights themselves lit a spark within him.

We read from the Torah, discussed what we read—and read again. My father questioned me and I questioned him. We were two scholars that night, traveling through the Torah together. Then suddenly my father said, "Mendel, the day is not far off when you will be a *bar mitzvah*. The days will fly by as if on bird wings."

"Yes, Papa."

"Mendel, you are my only living child. Only you can pray for me when I am no longer in this world. You are my treasure. I know you will make me proud."

I said nothing. I wanted to tell my father how sorry I was that I often played when I told him I was studying. I wanted to say that yes, I *would* study hard, that I'd do anything in the world to make him think well of me. And I wanted to tell my father something else too. I wanted to say how much I loved him, whether he got the permit or not. But I felt so shy and tongue-tied by my love that I could only stare down at the open page before me.

Papa, misinterpreting my silence, said, "We must not be disappointed because of the permit, Mendel. We must not despair because we cannot have the things upon which others build their lives. We are looked after. God helped our ancestors in the wilderness. That same God still lives; and just as the moon shines down on our little roof, so does He tenderly look down upon us."

My father spoke comforting words, yet I was not comforted. Thinking of the violence I had seen in the marketplace, I said, "But Papa, God looks after us, yet we still suffer. We are poor and weak. Why couldn't God have made us strong?"

"We *are* strong," he answered.

"How are we strong?" I challenged.

"We are strong, for we have the power to make circles."

"Circles?" I stared at my father. "I don't understand."

With his fingertip my father traced the rim of his wine glass. "The world is a large circle, Mendel, a circle made up of circles. God made the earth a circle. A bubble is a circle, and so is a water drop. The closed circle has power, for it holds magic. A broken circle has nothing."

"Explain it to me, Papa."

My father stroked his black beard while his mind strolled through the Talmud. After a few moments he said, "We circle the bride and groom under the wedding canopy. We circle the grave at the cemetery and the corpse at the funeral. We gather protectively in a circle around the sickbed and when a baby is born. On *Simchas Torah* we dance in a circle holding the Torah high above our heads. And on that day we begin the yearly circle of reading the Torah. Only the closed circle, Mendel, has power, because only the closed circle can keep us whole."

"Do you mean keep evil spirits out?" I asked.

He took a sip of wine and said, "Yes, keep evil spirits out. On Shabbos we give thanks for the life that grows on earth to sustain us, for the bread, for the wine. All growing things live and die in a circle we call a cycle. We eat food, and from the food's strength we are able to plant again, renewing what we have eaten. That too, Mendel, is a circle. On *Purim* and on *Pesach* we give thanks for the survival of our ancestors thousands of years ago. Our minds and hearts travel back along a road to the past to remember people in a way that makes them alive for us once more. This road is a circle. We are connected to those ancient people as they are connected to us. If we do not remember them, then the circle is broken; and a broken circle, Mendel, gives no protection, for it has no power. No power at all."

The candles now burned low. Papa's face was illuminated in a small ring of golden light. He poured a glass of sweet wine for himself and a few drops for me.

"Two thousand years ago a wise man believed evil spirits have no power in a sacred area. Whenever he asked God for rain, he drew a circle around himself. This was his own sacred area. All his power lay within it. No demon could enter the circle, and because of this, he became a great rainmaker . . . a great miracle worker. His name was Honi, but the people called him Honi Ha Me'a gel—Honi the Circlemaker. He knew the secret of keeping the power within his circle. He knew the secret of the unbroken circle."

"But Papa," I said, "do you mean we should all draw circles around ourselves?"

"No, but we can complete other kinds of circles, Mendel. Even now, as I talk to you, I am closing a circle. My knowledge is part of a circle from my grandfather through my father to me . . . and now to you. When you have learned it and when you have lived it, then you will have become as wise as my grandfather. For it is when you *give* that you gain power. Only then the circle closes. Only then do you become a circlemaker."

The candlelight was so dim now, I could hardly see Papa's face. Mama had fallen asleep. Our hut was still. My father stood up and began to pray. I stared at the night outside our window. The sky hung silent with a million stars. Papa is right, I thought. Nothing is really unconnected. Nothing exists alone. The stars formed circles, and the planets too. In the solar system they circled the sun, while smaller moons circled them. Even as I watched the heavens, my own earth was completing its circle around the sun. I felt it that Shabbos night as never before. I was part of this universe. Perhaps I too would become a circlemaker.

9

"Mendel! Mendel! Quick! You must come quick!" It was Wednesday afternoon. My father was away loading turnips in Smalnysk for a last delivery to the count, and my mother was working for Gittel, doing her laundry. My parents gone, I was on my way to Zalman's, racing over the dried mud path that led to his hut.

"Mendel, stop! Stop!" Chaim had spotted me and was calling and waving his arms wildly.

I hadn't seen or heard from Zalman in two days and couldn't wait to see him. "I can't come!" I called back. "I'm busy!"

But Chaim ran after me; his big eyes were filled with terror, and his head bobbed in that nervous way of his. "Come, Mendel, you must come! You must see it for yourself!"

"See what?" I asked, but he had started to run on. Drawn in by his panic, I followed him. We ran until we reached the market square where a crowd of people was pushing and shoving noisily to see something. What was it? Being thin and fast, I slithered quickly through the crowd until I was right in front of a large notice written in both Russian and Yiddish.

CONSCRIPTION NOTICE

BY AUTHORITY OF CZAR NICHOLAS, THROUGH WHOM THE VOICE OF GOD COMMANDS, THE FAMILIES OF MOLOVSK ARE TO PRESENT THEIR SONS, AGE 12 AND ABOVE, FOR INSPECTION AND INDUCTION INTO THE MILITARY, BE-TWEEN THE HOURS OF 8 AND 4 ON WEDNESDAY, THE 21st OF JULY, 1852, IN THE MARKET SQUARE.

TERM OF CONSCRIPTION IS 25 YEARS.

FAILURE OF FAMILIES TO APPEAR WILL RESULT IN A 3,000-RUBLE FINE PER FAMILY, AND PUN-ISHMENT.

FOR EVERY MISSING JEWISH BOY, UP TO 3 YOUNGER SIBLINGS MAY BE TAKEN.

ANYONE WHO HIDES A RUNAWAY WILL HIM-SELF BE CONSCRIPTED.

ANY JEWISH BOY, AGE 12 OR OVER, WILL BE SEIZED AS A CRIMINAL AND IMMEDIATELY CONSCRIPTED IF FOUND AWAY FROM HOME WITHOUT A GOVERNOR'S PERMIT.

The crowd around me was shouting. Housewives who had run from their huts to see the notice wailed loudly to each other. Chaim came up next to me, talking fast. "We've got to go, Mendel, we've all got to go into the army! Dovid . . . Dovid . . ."

"Dovid what?" I demanded impatiently as Chaim stuttered.

"Dovid . . . Dovid's been taken! Just moments ago!"

Dovid taken? I could hardly believe what I heard. I hated Dovid; yet I felt no joy at this news.

"Next it will be us! They are picking boys off the streets!" Chaim cried uncontrollably, tears streaming down his pale cheeks. I know it was cruel, but right then I ran from him, leaving him alone in his anguish.

I had to warn Zalman. I had to warn Zalman right away and then . . . ? Then I would think what to do! The narrow streets of the village were a mass of people. Soldiers on horseback trotted up and down, and their pistols and whips at the ready were a warning to the frantic crowds of Jews that milled about, panicked.

As I ran, I heard shots ring out—I dared not turn around. I ran faster than I'd ever run before. I heard the gallop of horses, shouts, more shots, but I kept on running until I reached Zalman's hut. I dashed to the door and banged on it furiously. No answer. I ran to the window and peered in. Empty!

No one at all. Dirty plates on the table but the food gone! And the bedding gone too! They'd left in a hurry. Escaped! I ran to the back of their hut. A dozen chickens fluttered out of my way. Their animals were untethered; the old cow and the little goat looked at me stupidly, not even aware of their freedom. Zalman and his family were gone! I was about to run when suddenly I heard voices—Russian voices! I looked around, and seeing a large empty barrel, I climbed inside it. Through the cracks in the slats I could see two soldiers on horseback. They rode right up to the hut, dismounted, and banged on the door. When they got no answer, they kicked it in with their boots. They were looking for loot, but as the hut was empty, they came out with nothing.

The soldiers talked loudly to each other in Russian, and I understood all of it. They were angry there was nothing to take, and they cursed. One of the soldiers lit a cigarette, then threw the match onto the thatch roof. I watched in horror as the small flame grew and grew, quickly engulfing one whole side of Zalman's home. The chickens squawked in fright. I saw the soldiers walk toward me. The barrel I was in had no lid. All they needed to do was glance down to see me. I held my breath and prayed they wouldn't. My prayer was answered, for they walked right past me.

I heard a shot and then another and another and another. They were shooting the animals! I heard them kill the cow, the goat, and for sport they used the chickens as moving targets. I covered my mouth with my hands, as I was afraid I'd cry out. I remained this way for several minutes. The burning hut made a terrible popping sound. I feared that at any second the barrel too would catch fire. I heard the loud talk of the soldiers as they mounted their horses and then the sound of horse hooves galloping away.

For several minutes I waited. All around me swirled the hot billowing smoke of the burning straw. Then I remembered it! With my eyes watering badly, I climbed out of the barrel. I rolled it quickly across the yard, around the dead chickens. I stood the barrel on end in front of the window of the burning hut and climbed on top. Then I pushed my hand through the smoking straw, coughing and groping, until at last my fingers closed around the leather case holding Zalman's knife.

10

From Zalman's hut I ran down to the river and along the muddy bank. My hand was burned, not bad—but enough to make it hurt; so as I went, I stuck it into the river to cool the pain. My mind raced back and forth as I tried to figure out what to do next. I knew I would not be overlooked. Tonight the soldiers would search every home to find Jewish boys. I had only two choices: stay and have my parents bribe the soldiers, or escape. My parents would want to use our bribe money, but it wasn't much . . . and if it didn't work? We all had heard stories of soldiers taking the bribe money, turning the boy over to the army anyway, then punishing the parents for trying to corrupt them! And if the bribe worked . . . what about the *next* time a conscription notice went up? Now that my father could not deliver for Count Oroskoff, we'd be lucky if we had money for food, let alone for bribery.

Besides, the result of a failed bribe was too terrible

for me to consider: twenty-five years in the czar's army—twenty-five years of not seeing my parents, ever. And them not seeing me or even knowing whether I was alive. And worse even than that was the cruelty done to Jewish soldiers. The spring peddlers had often talked of the isolation. The whippings. The starvation.

When I got to my hut, it was empty. Perhaps it was being alone in that little hut, alone and responsible only for myself, that brought the idea into my mind. I went to the carved wooden chest in the corner, took out some of the bribe money—100 rubles—and stuffed the silver coins deep within my pocket. I also took the last letter Aunt Bella had sent, her address written small at the top. I removed my prayer shawl from around my waist and laid it in the chest. Then I went to our cupboard and wrapped cheese and bread in a handkerchief, for I knew what I would do. I would leave. I would cross the Green Border and go where others had gone, to America. I knew that the czar's recruiters would be combing the countryside, hunting down runaways. We called them "trappers," but their prey was not forest animals —it was Jews. And for every Jew caught, the reward was 300 rubles. As much as I feared the trappers, I had to go. My parents will never see me be taken into the Cantonist army, I vowed.

Never!

And they will never be put in the danger of having to bribe a soldier.

Never!

I took the iron shears from my mother's sewing basket and cut off my earlocks. With this affront to God, I was confirmed in my decision.

HORSEHOOVES! I stood frozen at the sound. Then after a moment I realized it was the familiar rhythm of Taki pulling the cart home. My father drove the cart to the side of the hut. From Smalnysk he always came home around the back of the graveyard to get up our hill. Because of his route he probably was unaware of the violence down in the village. I knew he was only coming home briefly, for he had to bring the count his last turnip delivery, return the horse and cart, then walk the long way back.

I looked around the room. My eyes fell on my worn notebook. I tore a page from it and wrote:

> *Mama and Papa,*
>
> *I have gone to be with Aunt Bella. I will write you, and I will be safe. Don't worry. Please don't worry.*
>
> > *Your son,*
> > *Mendel*
>
> P.S. *Mama, do you remember when you told me that there comes a time when what I am now, and what I will be, meet? That time is now.*

I placed the note on the table and went to the door. I opened it just enough so I could see Papa. He had given Taki her feed bag and was now pumping water into the tub for her. I watched him cover the turnips with the gray canvas, knotting it tightly at the corners of the cart so they wouldn't fall out. Then he went back into the shed for something. Now was my chance! I ran to the cart, climbed up the back, swung my legs over, and squeezed under the canvas. I breathed in the soil-damp smell of the turnips as I pressed in among them. Not long after, I felt beneath me the unsteady bumping of wooden wheels along a dirt road.

The distance to Count Oroskoff's was only six *versts*. But it was six versts of danger. My father had a letter from the count giving permission for him to convey the turnips for this day, but now even letters of counts carried little weight against the czar's mandate. What's more, by hiding in the cart I was putting my father in great danger. From beneath the cloth I peeked fearfully out at the road, my heart beating like a quickly marching soldier. Praise God, though, we encountered no trouble; and about an hour after we left, I felt the cart veer as it turned up the broad carriage road of the Oroskoff estate. My father drove right to the count's huge store-house. He climbed down from the cart and went inside to talk to the overseer. It was then I looked out from under the canvas, and seeing no one about, I slipped down and hid in a row of bushes at the side of the road. Moments later, a young man came out to unload the turnips. Then when the cart was emptied, I saw my father climb back up and drive it down the long, straight path to the stable.

From the bushes I watched as the wobbly cart rolled away, growing smaller with every turning of the wheels, until at last it became no more than a tiny speck. Was that tiny speck at the end of the count's road . . . was that the last memory I'd ever have of my papa?

I stood up and looked around. No one in sight. With a breaking heart I began walking toward Pinski forest.

11

As I walked along the road, the dust curled upward from my shoes and settled again silently behind me. There was a stillness to the afternoon. Birch and oak trees stood unmoved by the lack of a breeze, and the fields of rye lay brown and motionless as a floor. The immobility of that afternoon seemed somehow fitting— my fateful day preserved from the breath of the world.

With my father I had ridden along country roads, but never walked along one. Now I felt so small and unprotected. At first I kept my head down, but after a while I let myself gaze across the wide fields.

Everything I saw was strange to me. The peasants arching their scythes high in the air to cut the stems of the rye plants, or raising their hoes to deliver the short, hard blows that loosened the turf from the ground. Women gathering muddy potatoes into their aprons while their babies played in the furrows. And the peasant boys driving the cows from the paddocks, singing to them in high voices while beating them quickly with long branches. These rough farm activities on the open stretches of soil fascinated me. I felt both drawn to and puzzled by them—like someone who enjoys yet cannot do the curious dances of another province.

By sundown I'd arrived at the edge of Pinski forest. So far it had been easy. In my rough clothes and with my shorn hair, I must have looked like a peasant boy, for no one thought me odd. Ox-cart drivers passed me with no more than the customary good-day greeting: "Daw Breedun!"

I sat down near a thicket of wild raspberries. I took out a chunk of the bread, said my prayers, and ate, plucking the raspberries and piling them on the bread like a sort of jam. Then I lay down on a thin layer of pine needles. The sky filled with stars. A breeze came up, and the small sounds of the world grew large. Squirrels scurried through the leaves, gnats buzzed near my face. And under the earth I thought I heard the tiny chattering of insects.

Soon the breeze blew stronger. Against the darkening sky I saw branches sway like giant arms, and I heard tree trunks creak with the sound of bones cracking. Remembering the Evil Eye and his love for the night, I shut my eyes tightly. An owl hooted; and suddenly, strangely, I saw how my mother's cheerless face looked when she was cutting noodle dough, and I began to cry. I was afraid of the dark, the unknown, and being alone.

I cried from fear and loneliness, and I cried for what I loved most that would never ever be again—my life in Molovsk. I cried until I could cry no more. Then slowly Zalman's words came into my head: "Maybe one day we'll meet in America." Perhaps I would meet Zalman there one day . . . and my parents too. Perhaps they would, in the end, see that America could offer a better life. This idea comforted me; so I thought it over and over again until the moon came up, large and yellow as a great wheel of cheese. And at last, exhausted, I fell asleep.

The Talmud describes dawn as the time when a dog can be distinguished from a wolf. When I woke, I could barely see my hand in front of me, yet I was so cold that I wanted to be off before dawn, rather than lie anymore on the damp forest floor. I got up and followed the path that led through the forest. As I went, the sun rose, splintering the light into yellow shafts, here lighting a fern, there brightening a clump of moss. I walked quickly, breathing in the wood smells. Was this the forest I feared last night? If I am to get to America, I thought, I must not be a baby, and right then I vowed never to cry again.

Soon I came to a clearing through which a brook flowed. I washed my hands of the night spirits, said my morning prayers, and walked on.

I had no idea how many versts it was through the forest, but I knew a horsedrawn cart went through it to

Pereginsko in a day and a half, so I figured I could walk through it in three. A trail was cut through the forest, and I followed this, though I walked beside it rather than on it so I could quickly hide in a thicket if I saw other travelers.

I feared seeing anyone now. It was well known that rich rewards could be won for turning in Jews trying to escape the military. Jews had been turned in by agents of the czar posing as revolutionaries. Even more horrible, they had been turned in by other Jews who themselves were conscripted but could supply a substitute to serve for them.

The forests were regularly scoured by all sorts of heartless trappers. I was so afraid of encountering one that whenever I caught sight of anyone—an old woman gathering mushrooms, a family of peasants in a hay wagon, or a deer hunter—I hid myself, remaining still and silent long after they were gone.

That second day passed uneventfully, but that evening, just after I had bedded down near a thicket, I heard a slow rustling nearby, as if someone was walking stealthily in my direction. I lay very still as the noise came closer and closer. In the twilight I could make out only a large moving shape, and now I saw this shape trudge directly toward me! In a moment I saw in the dim light two brown eyes staring down at me. A bear! In terror I shut my eyes tight and lay still as a corpse. Silently I recited all the prayers I could remember. The bear sniffed my head. Finally, just when I thought I could stand it no longer, he made a strange low growl and lumbered off. I could not sleep for hours after that. In the morning, however, the encounter with the bear amused me, and I dramatized it in my mind, making the bear bigger and myself braver, just as I might tell the incident one day to Zalman.

The third day I must have made good time. For even though my legs were sore, I stopped only briefly. And, curiously, whenever I did stop, I found myself looking up into the pine trees. I'd never seen so many tall trees together. Their crowded branches divided the summer sky into small irregular shapes, like pieces of broken blue glass. And for some reason that I didn't understand, the beauty of these trees, and especially the view of the sky seen through them, comforted me.

That third night was Shabbos. I washed in a stream and said my prayers for this special time. What were my parents doing tonight? I wondered. I pictured my father bending over the Torah in fading light and my mother praying silently. Praying for me. Tears stung my eyes at this image but I forced myself to think of other things, for I didn't want to cry.

I lay down by the stream and slept fitfully, dreaming of bears. When I woke on that fourth day, I was very hungry but decided to keep the last bit of bread and cheese as a reward for finishing the walk.

As I went on my last versts out of the forest, I thought over my plan. First I needed to find Valdi. I remembered Gittel saying that he could be found at several places, including the Pereginsko train station. This was my plan: I would go to the train station each day for a week until I spotted him. I knew what to look for. I had heard it said that he was bald, with only a ring of brown hair, that he was stocky and had a curious limp. Surely if I were alert I would find him. And if I didn't find him after several days? Then somehow I'd get across the border myself.

As I entered Pereginsko, I was sobered by this thought: Whether I lived or died was now up to me.

12

Pereginsko was a poor place. A teahouse, a bathhouse, and a few shops dotted the town haphazardly. I found the usual cluster of thatched-roof huts and a tiny church. Pereginsko seemed a ridiculously insignificant town to have the honor of a railway station. But it was given a station because of its nearness to many wealthy country estates. Noble ladies and gentlemen returning to Odessa or traveling to the border were obliged to use the Pereginsko station.

When I reached the train station, I stared in amazement. I had never seen a train station before, and it seemed to me now raucous as a marketplace. Besides the nobility, the station had a ragged supply of day workers, peddlers, peasants, and gypsies overflowing the platform in noisy mobs. I stood among people of all sorts who were running, tripping over baggage, and pushing each other. Soldiers gathered in large groups, smoking long brown cigarettes and shouting with laughter. How would I find Valdi in such a place? I wondered.

My legs were very tired now, but I didn't know if I should sit down. If I sat down, would I look less or more suspicious? At last I decided to squeeze myself into a small space on one of the benches outside the third class waiting room. I wedged myself between a large peasant woman whose dark hair was braided with red ribbons and an old man who leaned on a birch cane and muttered to himself. In front of us squatted a group of shiny-haired gypsy women playing cards and spitting tobacco. Further up on the second-class platform some merchants had opened their leather valises to the delight of a small crowd who fingered their wares. "Cotton socks from America!" they cried. "Silk undergarments from St. Petersburg!" A policeman tried to break up the on-lookers, but after a few minutes they regrouped again, ready to bargain.

I sat on the bench for a while, watching all this, when a train pulled into the station. I stared, fascinated, for I'd never seen a train. It was a string of long metal carriages, all connected, and with a chimney on top. The carriages had regular doors as rooms do, and now several people stepped out of them onto the platform. Most of the passengers were soldiers lugging muskets, but there was one man who caught my attention. He was bald, wore a frock coat, and carried what looked like a brand-new valise. I watched him walk toward the station house, and my heart gave a leap at the sight of the clubfoot that he dragged ever so slowly behind his good one. Valdi! It must be! This was Valdi! I had to act fast!

I pushed my way through the throngs of people on the platform. All the while I kept my eyes on him. I saw him go into the baggage room and followed him, accidentally bumping an old woman in my pursuit.

When I was right behind him, I suddenly realized I didn't know what to say to him exactly, but whatever I said it was only safe to say it in Russian. "Excuse me," I started, "I am traveling and need your help." The man looked at me as someone might look at an annoying beggar and turned away. I felt a sudden fear then but thought that perhaps it was only his caution that prevented him from readily responding, so I tried another tactic. "But I know who you are, Valdi, and I've come here to find you."

"I don't know what you're talking about, and I don't know who *you* are, nor do I care! Go away at once or I shall call for the stationmaster!"

The man had wheeled around to bark this at me. Trembling, I looked up into his angry eyes. I mumbled some apology and hurried out of the station house and down the platform.

"Where are you scurrying, little mouse?" Two rough hands grabbed my shoulders and a harsh voice growled into my ear, "And where's your Governor's Permit? Show it at once!"

13

I was violently spun around and found myself looking up at the stationmaster. He stared down at me with bloodshot eyes and a sneer curling on his lips.

"Please sir," I stuttered in Russian, "I . . . I'm only waiting . . ."

"Waiting, loafing, it's often the same thing to your sort. A little grandmother told me you tried to knock her down."

"Not me, sir."

"Well then, what have you been doing? Why are you running like a thief?"

"I am waiting . . ." I repeated feebly.

"Eh? Well, Mouse, for whom are you waiting? Eh? Speak up! And where is your Governor's Permit? Well, SPEAK UP!"

Terrified, I managed to say, "I . . . I'm waiting for . . . for . . . a relative."

"You're lying," the stationmaster snarled. "I can tell. C'mon, let's see your permit. Hurry up!"

"If you let go of me, I will get it for you," I said.

He let go, and then just as I was about to run as fast and as far as I could, I was grabbed again. A deep-throated Russian voice cried out, "Nicki! Nicki! It's a blessing to see you away from that old witch!"

The stationmaster and I both looked into the face of a short, squat man. A round face it was, with a gray stubble on the cheeks and a red web of veins on the nose. He was dressed like a peasant, for he wore a long, linen tunic over baggy trousers; and instead of shoes, he wore felt rags tied around his legs with twine.

"Excuse me, excuse me, please. A stone melts in my heart at the sight of my nephew. Poor orphan! I am taking him to his aunt in Werpl. Saints preserve her for taking in the lamb, and after his stepmother had treated the child so poorly. Nicki Nickolovitch, let your uncle Dmitri look at you! Not much fat meat on these bones . . . eh, officer?"

The man opened his mouth to laugh, exposing a row of teeth, gray and chipped as old tombstones. The stationmaster was not affected by the man's joviality.

"Where is his Governor's Permit?" he demanded.

"Oh, you don't need to see his permit! As I said, he will not be going out of Russia, only to Werpl at the border."

"Show me the permit!" the stationmaster bellowed. "Show it at once!"

The man fidgeted in each of his pockets, first slapping one noisily, then digging into it with much spluttering and fumbling until, at last, he pulled out a yellow paper scribbled with black ink and affixed with some sort of seal. While the stationmaster looked it over, the man continued to chatter.

"And didn't my sister warn me? 'Dmitri Nickolovitch, if you lose or tear that child's identification paper, then even the heavens can't intercede for him. The czar's men are no fools,' she said. 'They can spot a Jew or a gypsy in an overgrown wheat field! Nicki's a good Christian boy, but still he needs his papers.' Ho! Sometimes the old woman is stronger than a Cossack! It was just the other day she was saying . . ."

There was no chance for him to finish, for just then a train whistle could be heard, and the platform became a flurry of arms waving and legs running in all directions. Sleepy children awoke crying and were lifted onto shoulders; chickens squawked loudly as their cages were hoisted off the ground. The first-class passengers emerged from their waiting room, their porters hurrying ahead. The poorer passengers formed a big noisy crowd.

The stationmaster handed the yellow paper to me, saying, "Don't lose this and next time, speak more directly. You've wasted my time."

"I'm sorry," I said, then realized in horror that I had apologized in Yiddish!

I was a fool, but a lucky one, for as the train pulled in, my "Zeit mir moychel" was completely drowned by its shrill whistle, screeching brakes, and hissing steam.

The man whom I now realized must be Valdi snatched the paper quickly out of my hand, wheeled me around, then pulled me toward one of the train carriages. It was surprising how quickly this plump man could move. I was propelled so fast I barely felt my feet touch the ground.

As we came near one of the closed metal doors of the train, the man whispered, "Your name is Nickolai Nickolovitch. Don't talk unless spoken to—and then only in Russian. You can speak some . . . yes?"

"Yes."

"Good."

The door opened, and I found myself squeezed and twisted by the pushing mob behind me. Someone stepped on my toes, and when I tried to get a foothold on the first iron step, someone else jabbed me hard in the ribs. I winced in pain, then suddenly felt myself being lifted like a reluctant toddler and planted firmly on the top step. One last push from the swelling crowd at my back and I was inside the dark, cool, wood-slatted train carriage, breathing in the combined smells of sweat, smoke, and live chickens.

The benches filled up fast. I grabbed a seat with my back to the window and caught my breath as more third-class passengers stumbled, shoved, and squeezed their way inside. When everyone was in, pressed together, most crouching on their belongings in the center, I saw Valdi leap on. Without saying a word he handed me a gray ticket and settled himself on his own small bundle in the middle of the car.

I wanted to ask how long the ride would be, and more important, where I was going. But just then a blue-suited man clanged the door shut, and there came the jerky feel of the brakes being released. A small noise rose from the passengers, a sort of collective sigh, as the Pereginsko station slipped away behind us.

As the train sped on, a terrible thought crossed my mind. This man who rescued me from the station officer, this man who I, with no permit, blindly followed onto the train—this man who I so quickly assumed to be Valdi, was not bald and did not limp.

14

The thought that the man who posed as my uncle was not Valdi, but a trapper, filled me with terror. Yet how in the world could I know the truth? I leaned back against the bench of the train. "God," I prayed silently, "my fate is in your hands. Help me!"

I sat in misery while all about me there was an atmosphere of excitement. As soon as the train had made its first lurch forward, women began to unwrap sausages, cheese, and dried fish. Some nursed their babies, and others cleaned their children's faces with spit-dampened handkerchiefs. No one was idle. The young men began a card game while a few older ones loudly swapped stories. "Valdi" sat with this older group, and I watched him closely. He listened intently to everything the other men said and laughed heartily. He seemed entirely unconscious of me, as if the whole bizarre dialogue with the stationmaster had never happened.

I was surprised how fast a train went. I sat stiffly as it roared on. I wondered how, going so fast, it could stay on the rails. After a while I relaxed a little, and when I did, I saw with surprise that I was sitting next to the same dark-haired peasant woman I had sat next to at the station. She was asleep.

I took out the last of my bread. It was wood-hard, but I put the remaining pebbles of cheese on it and ate hungrily. The woman woke and drew out a little glass bowl of chicken livers, which she balanced on her lap. She beckoned me to eat. The temptation was great. The livers had the rich, fat smell I so loved; but I could eat only kosher meat, so I thanked her but pointed to my own chunk of bread.

"Ticket inspection! Ticket inspection! Have your tickets ready at once!" the blue-suited conductor shouted as he entered the car.

Many people had fallen asleep. Curled in grotesque attitudes formed by their cramped condition, they slowly awoke, then began digging into their bundles or their clothes for tickets. One young woman was questioned repeatedly, and a small group around her tried to explain something to the conductor. The scene made everyone nervous. Tickets were dropped on the floor, and a desperate kind of explaining accompanied almost all inspections. When the conductor stood before me, I handed my ticket to him. He tore off the right corner while searching my face, as if looking for something particular in it. I felt "Valdi's" eyes on me as well, and suddenly I heard myself say in flawless Russian, "Please, how far to Werpl?" The conductor snapped out of his reverie and barked, "About five hours."

After a while we felt the jolts and screeches of the train stopping. "Libosk station!" a voice called out.

This was not a regular passenger stop but a stop to unload freight headed for the south. Passengers could, if they wished, stretch their legs or buy food from the vendors. Even before the doors opened, a ragtag group of peddlers banged on the train windows and gathered outside the doors, hawking sesame rolls, *piroshki*, and fruit. For a kopek you could get a tin dipperful of hot tea.

The first-class passengers did not disembark, as they were comfortably eating in their dining car, but the second- and third-class passengers stumbled out of the steaming train into the cool sunlight. I saw "Valdi" motion for me to follow him.

I followed him off the train, but refused his offer to buy me an apple. This was my plan: to get back on the train alone, and if anyone asked, deny I'd ever met him. I would make up a story about visiting relatives, and if asked for my Governor's Permit, I'd say he stole it from me. I would avoid being associated with this man, for I had no proof he was Valdi or that he meant well for me. I preferred the danger of escaping alone to the danger of being caught by a trapper.

The conductor blew his whistle, and the passengers began hurrying back to the train. I was at the back of one of the freight sheds, using the bushes as a toilet. When I heard the whistle, I walked around the side of the shed toward the train; but in an instant I felt a warm breath on my neck and "Valdi's" voice command, "Turn around and walk slowly into the freight shed. Don't look over your shoulder! Don't make a noise! Don't stop!"

My heart raced, and the wildest thoughts spun in my head. I ignored his words and continued toward the train. Then it happened: His sweaty hand clamped over my mouth, and I was dragged quickly backward into a suffocating blackness.

15

In the darkness my arms were held tightly behind my back with one strong hand, and my mouth was clamped shut with another. I heard a long whistle and then the steady grinding rhythm of the train steaming away. As soon as the noise died in the distance, I felt a hard slap on my back. "Congratulations!" The hand was removed from my mouth, and just then a lamp was lit. I looked up into "Valdi's" grinning face.

"Little scarecrow, you made your first escape—with help from me, of course!"

His arrogant grin enraged me. "Escape from what?" I demanded.

"Escape from a train taking you to a real border with a customs office."

"So where am I now?" I asked, trying to sound un-afraid.

"Where are you? To be precise, you are in the freight

handler's office of the Libosk station. You'll stay here until midnight. There are no more trains through here today, so we will be left completely alone. Tonight you'll make your second escape."

"To where?"

"Ah, boy, the border is green and so are you. Don't you know we're only forty-seven versts from the border? Tonight we'll travel over the Carpathian Mountains to a farm about twenty versts from here, and from there you will travel through the woods, coming within six versts of the border station. Now, however, you'll rest here. Here you are safe."

"Then why are you holding me?" I asked defiantly.

This man who all the while had been gripping my arm now let go, threw his head back, and laughed like a fool.

There was a tiny alcove in this freight handling room, and while he was in his merriment, I saw a tall, thin man emerge from the alcove dressed in a freight handler's uniform. The man looked at us with cunning eyes that were like thin slits.

"Valdi" gained control of himself and turned in the man's direction. "Ivan, meet Nicki!" he cried. This man Ivan lifted his hat in the peasant manner, but said not a word. "Make tea, Ivan," commanded "Valdi," and like a servant the man went to a tarnished brass pot and put it on the small, coal stove that warmed the freight room.

"Were you looking for me at the station?" I asked. "How do you know I want to cross the border? Who are you? Is your name Valdi?"

He was placing some empty brandy crates near the stove. He turned and grinned at me, saying, "Too much curiosity is a bad thing, especially for boys. Sit down. I will only tell you that I see many things others don't. I see you're all alone; yet you're not an orphan. I see from your accent you're a Jew. I see you're of conscription age. I see you didn't know half the danger you were in with the stationmaster, nor the danger you're in now. So don't ask any more questions. If you want to call me Valdi, be my guest. I will tell you many things, but I will not tell you everything. So when I say one word, understand two." He sat down on one of the crates and gestured for me to sit on the other.

"Then you are Valdi, aren't you?" I asked stubbornly. He did not answer. I knew then he truly was not going to answer any more questions, so I remained silent. He poured two glasses of tea, and while we drank, he told me that he would help me cross the border.

"Trappers are everywhere, but I know a route through Turgov forest that is pathless and so heavily wooded that you'll be hard to find."

"But what if I am found?" I asked.

"Then speak only Russian. Show them the permit I have for you and make up a story. Say you wandered away from the train or somewhere. Say you did not get back in time and then got lost. Make up any fairy tale you wish, but remember this—if you want to strengthen a lie, mix it with a little truth. Of course, this is all easier if you are caught alone. To be caught with another is much more dangerous. *Two* Jews walking through the Turgov forest? An innocent broth is hard to ladle from these ingredients."

"Then you are Jewish too?" I asked.

"Me?" Valdi hooted.

I was afraid he was going to start his laughing again, so I quickly added, "You said, '*Two* Jews walking through the Turgov forest . . .' "

"I did," Valdi howled, "but not me! After tomorrow you will not see me again. You will travel with another of your kind. We will meet up with him at a farmhouse tonight."

I thought about this for a moment and was comforted. Although Valdi spoke of the added danger, to escape with another was far less frightening to me than going alone. As if reading my thoughts, Valdi said, "Throughout your escape you will not be alone. You will have someone at your side to help you; yet remember, ultimately only *you* are responsible for your own safety. Only *you* are responsible for your life."

As the sun went down, we drank more glasses of tea, but no food appeared. I was very hungry but did not mention it, as I did not want Valdi to think me weak. While we drank, he told me the route I would take across the border. He said when I crossed it, I'd be in the Austrian Empire, but specifically I'd be in Hungary. Not far into Hungary was a farmhouse where I would be helped, and he even taught me a little poem to remember where it was. At last he said, "Here now is your permit." I put the wrinkled piece of paper in my pocket. "I will tell you more tomorrow morning," he said wearily. "That is all for now." He turned from me and began writing on coarse gray paper.

I stared nervously out at the dark sky while Ivan sat in the corner, chewing tobacco and at intervals spitting nastily into a tin spittoon. Hours passed. I couldn't relax. I felt as if I were drifting on a swiftly moving river but could neither anchor nor swim ashore. Everything I cared about and everything I knew was in a place to which I could never return. Now I was on a journey with strangers to unknown places, and the only familiar thing at all was myself.

Just as I was getting drowsy, Valdi steered me out the door and into an empty splintery cart harnessed to a dray horse. He climbed up onto the driver's bench and told me to climb in the back. The night hung dark and wet. I could almost drink its black air. I was wearing my jacket, but the wool was threadbare and I shivered. "Take my coat," Valdi suddenly said, turning around. He had on a thick sweater and could have done without the heavy coat, but as I still didn't completely trust him, I didn't want to be obliged to him for yet another thing.

"I'm not cold," I lied. He argued with me, but I was firm. When he turned back around, I covered my shoulders and legs with some burlap sacks that lay in the cart.

As we went, I wondered about so many things: Who was Ivan? Was he really a freight handler? And if so, why was he helping Valdi? Who was Valdi? Was he really an Idealist as Gittel had said? Would he ask payment from me for his help? Why was he doing this at all, and where was I going? How did he get a Governor's Permit? And how did he know I was in trouble at the station? The questions swam round and round in my head like fish in a pool, until I became so tired and cold I could think no more and fell asleep on the floor of the wagon.

We traveled over the mountains, and I slept fitfully the whole time. It was several hours later when I felt the wagon stop and heard the barking of a dog. A lantern swung in front of me, and I saw we were stopped at a farmhouse. Climbing down from the wagon, I now realized how very cold I was. My legs and arms could only move stiffly, like those of a doll. And when I opened my mouth to ask a question, my teeth chattered so badly I could not talk.

"Ah, boy, you'll need something hot in your belly," Valdi said, looking at me with concern. Taking off his wool coat, he wrapped it around me with such care that from that moment I began to trust him. With his help I staggered to the house. The door opened and a pretty blond-haired woman stood there, looking at us in surprise. Her eyes were blue as the cornflowers that grow at the edge of wheat fields.

"Czar's knickers!" she exclaimed irreverently. "You are bringing them younger each time!" She led us into a dimly lit kitchen heated by an enormous clay stove and bade us sit at a rough, oak table. Her home, like all peasant homes, had its "Beautiful Corner," a corner shelf with an icon of Saint Nicholas illuminated by a small candle. But unlike a peasant, Valdi did not bow before it on entering.

As soon as we sat down, she handed us each a wooden bowl of black bread—crumbled and soaked in hot milk with a great, brown lump of honey melting on top. I ate hungrily, for it seemed to me the most delicious thing I'd ever eaten.

"So, what do you say?" the woman asked Valdi in a teasing voice. "Will it be babies next, eh? What do you say?"

But she was not really looking for an answer, for in the next breath she said to him, "I want to warn you that even farms this side of the forest are being closely watched for border jumpers. Just last week two soldiers came around asking if I had seen anything suspicious."

"What did you say to them, Anna?" Valdi asked.

"I said, 'Suspicious? Excuse me, I'm just a peasant woman and am not so easy with large words. If you mean have I seen anything *strange*, then I'll tell you I haven't. My husband died three years ago, and isn't a widow's home the quietest of all? The strangest thing here,' I told them, 'was the mare birthing two colts in July.'"

"They wanted nothing more?" Valdi asked.

"No, the bastards, but they searched the house and barn as if looking for diamonds. They upset the animals so much the cow's milk was still coming late three days after they left!" As if jolted back to the present by this fact, the woman asked me, "How about more hot milk? Aren't your bones asking for some?"

"Yes, please," I croaked. While she poured milk into my bowl, she continued to talk excitedly to Valdi.

"I've heard that there's a good deal of rubles to be made turning in runaway conscripts, but the border guards want them first. All along the frontier the guards are looking for escapees. And now they say that three more units of guards are arriving Tuesday to patrol the border. The farmwives have been asked to board them for a night when they arrive."

Valdi said nothing, for he was deep in thought. The woman, taking a clue from his face, said softly, "I wish you success. Every escape is a victory for the people against the murderous regime of Czar Nicholas!"

Then, to my surprise, this pretty woman bent down and kissed Valdi tenderly on his cheek, and Valdi returned her kiss on the mouth. I stared down at my bowl, embarrassed. The room was silent. I could hear only the night chirping of grasshoppers out in the fields. At last Valdi turned to me and said, "You'll start your journey tomorrow. Now go and sleep. In the morning I will give you your final instructions."

The woman then rose, picked up the lantern, and beckoned me to follow her. I had hoped I would be sleeping in the warmth of the farmhouse, but I saw now they intended for me to sleep in the barn. The woman led the way to a wood building, shining gray in the moonlight. She put her lantern down as she slid the iron latch on the big door and opened it just enough for me to enter. In the darkness I heard a low mooing. The woman then picked up the lantern to lead me further inside. The barn was surprisingly warm and smelled pleasantly of cow dung, fresh hay, and pinewood. But even the warmth of the barn could not stop me from turning cold at what I saw in the dim blush of lantern light.

16

Asleep under a blanket in the haypile was the large, familiar figure of Dovid. My surprise was so great that I stood rooted to the barn floor, even when the woman handed me a blanket and told me to get to sleep. Only after she left did I move. I lay down on the straw along the opposite wall and pulled the blanket up close around my head as if to blank out his sight. As strange and puzzling as was the whole event with Valdi, this topped it. To see the Rag Rat here, *here* in the very barn to which I escaped was not only a shock, but bad luck. Was he the "someone" I was to always have at my side? The idea of going through the forest with this hateful bully made my stomach churn. While he slept, I thought bitterly of the bizarre ways God often works.

The hay had a sweet, spicy smell, as if newly cut. It was piled thick, and at my slightest turn crunched gently beneath me. After sleeping nights on hard, damp ground, this was heaven; yet I was so unsettled that I could not fall asleep. How could I cross the Green Border with Dovid? How could it possibly work? No, I thought over and over again, it couldn't. Yet, what can I do now? I wondered frantically. I can't go back!

I felt then I neither had the courage to go into the army nor the courage to cross the border with Dovid. What a coward I was! I tossed nervously all night. At last I decided that this awful arrangement with Dovid would have to work. It would just have to. Somehow.

I fell asleep toward morning, but not long afterward I felt a dull kick in my ribs and heard a voice ask, "K'vatsh! What are you doing here?"

I looked up into Dovid's face, seeing a horrible blue bruise above his left eye.

"What are *you* doing here?" I asked, ignoring his insult. "Chaim said you were taken into the army."

"I was," he replied, lifting his filthy tunic to show me the old soldier shirt he was wearing underneath.

"So how did you get here?" I asked.

"I escaped." Dovid answered nonchalantly, as if escaping from the army was an easy thing.

"You're lying," I said recklessly. "It's impossible to escape from the army!"

Dovid looked at me with his cold eyes; and for a moment I thought he was going to swing at me, but he just said, "It wasn't impossible for *me*."

I was about to ask him how, when the barn door opened and Valdi walked in. He was carrying two bowls of bread with hot milk, as I'd had the night before. Dovid and I sat on the straw and ate hungrily while Valdi talked.

"Good! You've gotten to know each other," he crowed. "That's a start. For the days ahead you'll need to trust each other more than brothers."

Neither Dovid nor I responded to Valdi's words. After an awkward moment I asked, "What will we eat?"

A smile flashed quickly across Valdi's face. "I have food for you in these packs." He handed us square, canvas back bags about the size of large prayer books. We each took one, and though I was tempted to open it right then to see what was inside, I resisted. As if reading my mind, Valdi said, "Don't worry, you will not find pork . . . or *kvass* either. For drink, try river water. Now listen carefully, for I have more than an hour's worth of information for you, and I will say it only once.

"The farm we're at sits just east of Turgov woods, and the entrance to the woods is twenty-seven versts from the Hungarian border. The border itself has no gate, no fence, no wall. Instead, every ten versts or so along the border there is a guardhouse with soldiers who watch for smugglers and border jumpers."

"How will we avoid the soldiers?" I asked.

"By moving silently, keeping your ears open, observing closely, acting fast . . . and of course," Valdi added, "being lucky."

"If the border is twenty-seven versts away, it should take us only two days to get to it. That's nothing," Dovid said.

"You must get there by *tomorrow*," Valdi replied dryly. "And there is no path to follow; it's a troublesome way. Not only is much of the land hilly, but it is thick with trees, and there are brooks to cross. You will need to understand at every moment where you are and where you're going. You'll have secret maps that show markers along the way; yet staying in the right direction will still be difficult.

"Now, listen. The border comes three versts after a long ravine that runs a verst or so along the frontier. To cross it, I've put a board along the width of the ravine in one place; you'll see it on the map. But beware that less than six versts south from that ravine crossing is a guardhouse. When you cross the ravine, go west, but be watchful! The ranks of the border guards are filled with scoundrels who, for a few kopeks, would shoot their mothers. They are looking for gun smugglers and spies along the border, but they are lazy and undisciplined—not even honest enough to bribe. Watch out for them; they're more brutal than *Tatars*." Valdi paused and looked into our faces, as if to see whether we understood. Then he continued in an urgent voice.

"I'm warning you—what is most important of all is that you get across the border *by tomorrow night*. That means before Tuesday, when the additional guard units arrive. The increase of guards will make it impossible to get through undetected, so remember, go quickly . . . or you will most certainly be discovered. Do you understand this?"

We nodded.

"Besides," Valdi added wryly, "by tomorrow night your food will be gone; so if you don't get shot, you'll starve."

"I've got experience escaping," Dovid said. "I should be the leader."

Valdi looked into Dovid's relentless eyes and after a moment said, "Yes, you be the leader; you are more experienced, as well as older and stronger."

I said nothing but my heart was burning with shame that I was so obviously weaker. I looked at Dovid, and he flashed me a smug grin. Perhaps Valdi caught that grin too, for he warned, "But as leader, you have to be wise—so remove that soldier shirt I know you've got on under your tunic—unless of course you *want* to be identified as a runaway from the czar's army."

When Dovid, embarrassed, had removed his shirt, Valdi said, "Now let me tell you about the maps."

But just then the barn door opened, and the woman walked in with a bucket to milk the cows, yet calling out in a strange, tense voice as of warning, "We have a visitor! Father Polgyana is here and needs help." A moment later an old, thin priest entered, his black robe sweeping along the hay-strewn floor.

The priest's face was gaunt and wrinkled, and his very long beard, gray and curly, hung like oak moss all the way to the large metal cross that dangled from a cord at his waist. "Christ be with you!" Valdi said, making the sign of the cross and bowing low before him in the

peasant fashion. I didn't cross myself but bowed and
Dovid, catching on, bowed as well.

The priest looked at us as if we were all curiosities;
then Valdi said, "Holy Father, I would be honored to
help you. Just tell me what I can do."

"I am on my way to a christening in Skorkov," the
priest answered, "but my horse has suddenly become
lame with a large pebble in its hoof. I removed the
pebble but the hoof is cut, and so my horse will be lame
for at least another day. This good woman has offered
to stable it here until the hoof heals, but still I must get
to Skorkov. Will you take me? I need to leave immediately."

Valdi hesitated, and the priest, perhaps sensing his
reluctance said, "It is only seven versts or so from here,
but I am an old man and cannot walk it."

"I'd be honored to take you, Good Father," Valdi
said. "I will take these farm boys down the road too, as
their work here ends today."

"Saint Nicholas bless you," said the priest.

"You two! Out the door! We leave immediately!"
Valdi shouted at us as if we were common field boys.

Valdi quickly hitched the dray horse to the cart; then
he ran back in the barn and came out with two light
sheepskin cloaks that the peasants wear, and a milking
stool. He threw a cloak at each of us, shouting as if in
anger, "You boys almost forgot your cloaks!" Then he
put the stool down, and Father Polgyana stood on it to
climb up to the driver's bench. Dovid and I clambered

into the back, while Valdi swung himself onto the bench beside the priest. He slapped the reins hard against the horse's flanks, and we were off.

What the priest and Valdi talked about I do not know, for the cart wheels were so creaky I couldn't hear. Once, though, I thought I heard Valdi tell Father Polgyana his name was Sergei, and several times I saw him cross himself to make a point. I sensed that even though the priest looked to be a kindly man, Valdi was making elaborate lies to disguise his identity. I figured Valdi had learned from experience to trust no one.

Dovid and I spoke not a word to each other. This abrupt departure cast a gloom over us both. We knew that Valdi had much more of importance to tell us— information that we would now have to go without.

After a short while we came to a fork in the road, and Valdi climbed down and motioned for us to get out. It was just at that moment that I remembered—we had yet to be given maps!

"Well, boys," Valdi said with fake cheeriness, "here you are. You can try the Petrosky orchard down the road; perhaps they could use hardworking boys like yourselves for their apple picking." Then he came around the back of the wagon and whispered, "The Turgov forest begins here on your left. Remember, go quickly!"

At this moment I whispered in panic to Valdi, "You never gave us our maps!"

For a long, long moment he said nothing as the priest

had now turned around to look at us, but at last Valdi cautiously said, "Yes, boys, don't you remember, *in your cloaks,* look in your cloaks!" Valdi threw his head back and laughed falsely. "Father Polgyana, these simple boys forgot where they put their wages!" Valdi continued to laugh horribly for several moments while the priest smiled charitably at us.

Valdi climbed back up onto the driver's bench and without giving us another look, steered the cart toward Skorkov.

After several minutes Dovid and I walked into Turgov forest, wearing our cloaks and carrying our food packs.

When we were well away from the road, Dovid commanded, "K'vatsh, get out your map. Let's not walk too far before we know we're going in the right direction."

I searched my cloak, but there was no map in it. "I don't have it," I said. "The map must be in yours."

"You hardly looked. Look again!"

"I don't have it!" I answered angrily, "so look in your cloak."

Dovid inspected his cloak, but he too found nothing.

"Let's look in the linings," I suggested. "Maybe the woman sewed the maps into the linings." The sheepskin cloaks were lined with thin wool, and so very carefully and slowly we felt all about the linings, checking for any abnormality—a bulge, a lump that would prove a paper was hidden inside. But though the cloaks were very crookedly and strangely stitched, the linings lay as smooth and flat as Shabbos tablecloths.

"Damn him!" Dovid cursed. "That bastard lied to us! We've got no maps at all!"

I didn't want to believe that Valdi would betray us, but I could find no other explanation for why he dumped us here without maps. "What'll we do now?" I said more to God than to Dovid, yet Dovid answered.

"I'm the leader, remember? I'll figure the way out somehow."

All courage left me then, and I felt hollow and hopeless. I realized the terrible foolishness of my decision to leave Molovsk. For now here I was, trying to cross a treacherous border that had claimed the lives of hundreds—me, a Jew, a runaway from the czar's conscription with little food, no map, and for my leader, Dovid.

17

Dovid stretched his arm out, pointing a way through the dense forest. "Hungary lies to the west, and the sun moves westward. So if we follow the movement of the sun, we'll get to the border." His reasoning seemed too simple; yet I had no better idea, so we began walking in the direction he had pointed. I felt then as aimless as one who jumps into the Dniester to reach Siberia.

As we went, I saw that Turgov forest was very different from Pinski forest. Pinski forest had open spaces, small lakes, and the trees were tall and grand. But this forest was thick with bushes and short pine trees whose branches arched low over us like protecting arms. The land was different too. Pinski forest was flat, but the land here swelled into hills, then dipped into shallow valleys. And all about, the boggy soil was black as peasant bread.

We walked on for hours, barely saying a word to each

other. How I wished then I was with Zalman instead of Dovid. I wanted to talk. I wanted to share my thoughts with someone, but Dovid either ignored my attempts at conversation or ridiculed whatever I said.

At last in desperation I asked, "How did you get that bruise over your eye?" Dovid usually had some bruise or other, as his father was known throughout Molovsk for his violent temper, and he beat Dovid as regularly as my father said prayers. But this bruise was worse than any I'd seen on him. It covered the whole area above his left eye and was blue as Cossack breeches. "Did you get that bruise in the army?" I asked.

Without looking at me, he said roughly, "I don't want to talk about it now." So we continued on many more hours in silence.

Descending into a shallow valley, we heard a rushing noise and soon came to a stream. The stream flowed quickly, and the water was so clean we could see colorful pebbles in it, clearly enlarged as if under glass. Feeling our luck then we knelt down, put our mouths to the stream and drank the water like animals. Then we sat on the bank, took our shoes off, and put our hot, tired feet in the cold swirling water.

When we had enough of the stream, we opened our food packs, and it was like opening gifts. Inside we each found a jar of herring, two apples, six slices of bread, a wedge of milk cheese, a small jar of salted cucumbers, and best of all, a small gray pot of honey with a wax stopper. I washed my hands in the stream, said my prayers, then ate. It was so good to find the stream and to have this food that, even with Dovid next to me, my spirits began to lift.

It was late afternoon, and I was very hungry. I ate two slices of bread, half a jar of herring, one apple, and a small slice of cheese. When I finished, I took out Zalman's knife, broke the wax seal on the honey and pulled out the cork stopper. The honey was soft and golden, and its sweet perfume reminded me of Gittel's bakery.

"Take your nose out of the honey; you look like a fool with your nose stuck in there."

"I was smelling Gittel's bakery," I said, then thinking a moment, added, "why did you steal my turnovers that day?"

Dovid gave a snorting sort of laugh. "I was hungry," he said. "They were good too, still warm."

"It's wrong to steal," I told him. "A thief is not much better than a murderer."

"Rot!"

"It's not rot! That's what the Talmud says and you know it!"

"Don't tell me what I know," he said. "I know more than you ever could. You're a sniveling baby, but I'm almost a man. You can't tell *me* about stealing and murdering, for I've done both."

"You have not!" I hooted. "You've stolen, but you haven't murdered! Where's the body if you've *murdered*?" I couldn't help myself then; maybe it was the good food or the cool water or just his ridiculous boast, but I started to laugh.

"It's near Ruchnick," he said.

"What is?" I asked.

"The body."

"Rot!" I said, sneering at him in just the way he'd sneered at me.

"If you shut your mouth," he said, "I'll tell you how it happened."

"Go on," I said.

Then very, very slowly, as one carries a bucket so no water splashes, Dovid told me how he escaped the army. Slowly and steadily he talked—so no emotion would spill into his tale.

"I was sorting rags for my father in the yard behind our hut that Wednesday—the day the conscription notice went up. A fat Latvian soldier rode up and asked me my name. I told him and he said, 'You're a big strapping fellow. Why are you doing this woman's work?'

" 'It's not woman's work,' I answered. 'I work for my father. He's a ragpicker.'

" 'Ragpicker! Nosepicker! It's the same worthless Jew sort of trade.' I ignored him and went on sorting.

" 'Why aren't you in the army?' he asked. 'It can't be because you're married. Who would ever marry a filthy fellow like yourself!' Then he laughed so heartily I thought his horse would break beneath his hog weight. When he stopped, I told him that, in fact, I was married;

for I knew that married boys don't get taken. 'You're a lying Jew!' he said. 'Look at you—a big strong boy trying to evade your duty. Come with me.'

"Then I told him a million things. That my wife was in Kherson visiting her mother; that I was really a Christian; that I needed to support my father; that I was about to go to university in St. Petersburg; that I had consumption. But he listened to nothing. He drove me ahead of him, his pistol pointed at my back. As I walked, I kept thinking of ways to escape, but the pistol kept me from trying.

"At one point on this march he stopped and asked slyly, 'Jewboy, perhaps if you really can't go, you have a thousand rubles to donate to the czar?'

"I had no money at all to bribe him with, not a kopek, let alone a thousand-ruble fortune, and at that moment I cursed those city Jews who easily can pay off these devils to save their darling sons.

"He marched me about two versts to the Verblovsky lumberyard. In the center of the yard stood a cart, the large kind used for lumber. But instead of lumber there were about forty boys inside, crammed like herrings in a crate. The cart had come up from the south, collecting these boys in the towns along the way. Their eyes were glassy with fever, and their lips were cracked."

"Did you know anyone in the cart?" I asked.

"From Molovsk I recognized only three. One was Chaim."

"Chaim!" I exclaimed. "I saw him that day! He must

have been caught in the streets just after you were taken!"

"He was caught right after me, and he was crying like the rest of them. You too would have been one of the crying babies. And it's a fact some of them *were* babies. Kalmen and his twin brother Yankel were in the cart."

"They're only eight!" I cried.

"That's right," Dovid said, "and they both bawled with the same pathetic voice. Now stop interrupting.

"In charge of our little 'battalion' were two men. The first was a short, dark man whose uniform was wrinkled and smelly. His name was Lieutenant Astafy. The second soldier, Ilya, was a tall, young one who slapped the faces of the crying boys. Lieutenant Astafy told us we were heading to the Vyatka garrison far away in the eastern cantons. As Cantonists we'd learn the Christian life until we were eighteen. Then we'd begin our twenty-five-year military service. When I heard him say this, I knew we were doomed, for I couldn't see how forty sick children in a lumber cart could possibly survive the 1500 versts to Vyatka. But when I looked into Astafy's cold eyes, I saw he didn't care a rat's tail if most of us died on the way." Dovid paused.

"Well?" I asked. "Then what happened?"

"You'll know soon enough," was his answer. He opened his jar of cucumbers and crudely poured them into his mouth. While I waited for Dovid to finish them, I lay on my back and looked up through the trees. The sun was still high in the sky. Every so often a cloud, white and fluffy as a featherbed, floated by. The warm forest air carried the tangy scent of pine, and there came at intervals a bird call that was like the pealing of a little bell.

Dovid ate every last cucumber, and next he drank the cucumber juice in big gulps. Then, in all this beauty, he continued his terrible tale.

18

"Not long after we started out, I realized I was right about Astafy. We were traveling very slowly. With all of our weight the cart could only bump sluggishly along the rough roads. Astafy and Ilya rode on horseback beside it. After several hours Astafy got off his horse and talked to the wagon driver. Then he shouted at us, ordering us out of the wagon. When we were all out, the driver turned the empty wagon around and left while the group of us stood there, hungry and miserable. Then we were made to walk, and for the next several hours we were herded like sheep along the dusty road. I knew what Astafy had done. He'd sent the driver away so he could pocket the money that was supposed to pay for our transport.

"We were forced to walk all that afternoon. It didn't bother me, though. I could have walked twice as far."

"But what about the younger ones?" I asked.

"They couldn't keep up, and when they stumbled and cut their knees, they felt the lash of Astafy's riding whip."

"How did you escape?"

"I'm coming to that. Shut up and listen. Toward nightfall we arrived at the Ruchnick garrison, a two-story stone building at the town's edge. The soldiers there dished up cod that was so salty not a boy could swallow it, for it was like eating plain salt. After this foul supper we were taken upstairs to the second-floor barracks, which were laid with straw mats, but no bedding at all. We were lined up beside these mats while Astafy gave us what he called a 'devotional lesson.'

"He went from boy to boy, and if one had a prayer shawl around his waist, he pulled it off him. He also took prayer books, amulets, and yarmulkes and dumped them all on the ground in a heap. He told us we would not be allowed to speak Yiddish ever again, nor to ever write or receive letters written in our language. About six of the boys were not Jews: Four were gypsies, and two were orphan boys, even skinnier than you. Astafy called us all godless and wicked. He said the czar was God's vicar on earth. And he said Czar Nicholas wanted us to be of pure heart, and that meant we had to be Christian. We would all have to convert, and it was better for us to do it soon. If we converted, we would eat mutton stew, cabbage soup, and plum tarts. But if we refused to convert, it would just be more salty cod. If we converted, we would sleep in real beds, maybe even with goosefeather coverings. If not, we would have only the cold mats on the stone floor. As Astafy told us all this, he smiled a lizard's smile, then made us all put on patched army shirts. After this he ordered us all to kneel on the hard floor and pray. About half of the boys did say the Christian prayers, and they immediately got to lie down; but the rest of us who wouldn't got a lashing with a birch rod and were forced to kneel for three hours, which Astafy said would 'give us inspiration to pray.' "

Dovid paused. Then prompted by the cruel memory, there appeared a look of terrible anger on his face. Very suddenly it came, as when a harsh wind pushes a cloud abruptly into the sky.

After several moments the look passed, and Dovid continued. "For hours the cold, stone building echoed with the sobs of the kneeling boys. Finally, very, very late, the boys keeled over and fell asleep. I only pretended to sleep, for I watched and waited. The younger soldier, the one they called Ilya, kept guard. He sat red-faced and upright in a chair, watching us all. Across his legs lay a rifle longer than a Cossack saber. He was young and strong, this Ilya, but I could tell he was stupid as an ass. All night I watched him, waiting for him to fall asleep, but he never did. Then I got an idea. I rose from the cold floor and walked toward him.

" 'I am very cold,' I said. 'Do you have a blanket?'

" 'A blanket!' he jeered. 'What do you think I am? A nursemaid?'

" 'Well,' I said, as if it was a terrific secret, 'I have ninety rubles, and I'll give it to you if you find me a blanket.'

" 'I don't believe you,' he snarled. 'Get back on the floor and lie down, or I'll call Lieutenant Astafy.'

" 'It's true,' I said, 'I *do* have ninety rubles. Here, you can take them.'

"I reached into my pocket and closed my left hand tightly in a fist around nothing. In the shadowy moonlit room he watched my hand slowly come out of my pocket, then he greedily grabbed for the fortune in it. Anticipating this movement, I caught him off guard. *Smack!* My tight fist caught his jaw in a hard bone-cracking punch. He reeled back. I grabbed the rifle. I had to act fast, for his fall overturned the chair, and the noise would bring the others running. As he stood up, I . . ."

"Did you shoot him?" I asked. "Did you?"

"No," Dovid said. "With both hands I held the rifle firmly by its barrel and brought the butt end cracking down on his head. Hard."

I shuddered at the horror of it, and Dovid looked at me with contempt, as if I were a faint-hearted girl.

"I killed him," he said matter-of-factly. "And some of the boys woke at the noise. One boy ran up to me, 'Take me with you!' he begged. I pushed him aside and ran to the open window. At first I thought I could climb down the tree outside, but it was too far from the window. So I had to jump, and though I broke no bones,

my head struck a branch as I went down. Just as I landed,
I saw the lights flickering in the barracks and heard the
cries and commotion inside. My head hurt like hell; yet
I ran as fast as I could, and when I came to Ruchnick,
I went straight to the synagogue. I found the rabbi there
getting ready for the morning prayers. He was shocked
at my bleeding head and the dirt on my clothes.

" 'I'm in trouble,' I said. 'Help me!' He asked me what
kind of trouble, and I told him how I had just escaped
from the army. 'Help me get to Pereginsko,' I said. 'I've
heard there's a man there who can get me across the
border.' The rabbi hesitated. Then he said, 'If I help
you and it is discovered, they will fine the whole Jewish
community here and flog us too, for that is the czar's
decree.'

" 'Don't help me, then,' I said. 'I don't need your
damned help!' I turned to leave, but he called me back.
'Wait, I have an idea.' He took me to the pump so I
could wash, and he gave me this woolen tunic to put
on. Then he led me through the back streets to a livery
stable. The man there was fitting up a carriage to deliver
to a wealthy family not far from Toldoski. He wasn't to
leave until the next day, but I saw the rabbi give him
five rubles for his trouble, and we left at once. On the
entire ride the man did not say a word, and I wondered
why he didn't question me. Did he know I was a Jew
traveling without a passport? Did he know I had escaped
from the army? Would he turn me in for the 300-ruble
reward? To figure him out I began a conversation, only

to find out he was deaf! I was in luck. We rode in high style up on the carriage ledge and went at a fast clip, for we were pulled by two fine mares. He shared his bread and sausage with me and let me drink some kvass too. In the evening we arrived in Toldoski."

"But how did you get to the farmhouse?" I asked.

"How do you think? By using my brain. I was walking through the streets of Toldoski when a young man came up to me. He was dressed as a peasant, but his talk was like a freethinker or an Idealist. He began to talk of pleasant things to me, and at first I didn't answer, for I thought he might be a trapper. But as he talked, his conversation became more and more dangerous. Russia was an old nest, he said, dried and falling apart. The czar he called a medieval tyrant. We could all be free souls if we followed the example of France or of democratic America and revolted against tyranny. All over Russia, he said, people would study the ways of free men and work for a new society. If I joined his group, he said, I would free my soul. I listened to him, then I risked telling the truth. I told him I was in great need. I said I too had no love for the czar, for I had just escaped from his army. For the love of freedom, I asked him if he knew anyone who could help me get across the border. He told me of a farmhouse about ten versts out of town, and he told me of the woman, Anna, an Idealist who housed border jumpers there. I walked without stopping all night until I found the farmhouse. The woman, Anna, took me in. On my third night there you arrived. You see, my whole escape was easy. I came through not only alive but richer."

From a pocket in his breeches Dovid pulled a five-ruble note.

"You stole it from the deaf man!"

"I need it more than he does," Dovid said simply.

I was so overwhelmed by this wicked deed that I said nothing. Then reflecting on the whole pitiful horror of Dovid's tale, I said, "What will happen to those boys in the barracks? What will happen to Kalmen and Yankel? And what will become of poor, simple Chaim!"

Irritated by thoughts of others, Dovid answered, "How would I know? Let *them* figure out a way to escape. I don't care a pig's snout about them. Their tears are only water to me!" Then, as if inspired by his words, Dovid got up and walked into the stream. He stripped off his shirt, cupped his hands full of water, and splashed his chest and back again and again.

While he was having his bath, I sat deep in thought. Why were people so hateful to each other? What was the point of it? I looked down at the sheepskin cloak. A line of ants was traveling along the seams as if on roads. Two of the ants carried a tiny crumb of cheese I had dropped, and the others hurried behind them. All the ants raced in the same direction. I watched them. Why can't we be like ants? I wondered. Why can't people help each other? After all, aren't we all on the same road that runs from birth to death? I looked at the ants more closely. Their tiny bodies maneuvered the lining's landscape with amazing strength. They traveled in groups over heavy stitches piled up like little hills and ran across a line of tiny knots, as if across a bridge.

The cloak was their countryside. To the ants the small mass of cut threads was dense bush, and the uneven black stitches along which they went meandered like a trail. A trail? I closely examined my cloak's lining. I grabbed Dovid's cloak and lay it flat next to mine and studied both linings together. Then I shouted with joy, "DOVID, WE'VE GOT A MAP!"

19

"Look, here is all of Turgov forest, and here is our route!" I pointed to the black road of stitches that ran from the left bottom corner of the cloak to the top right. "See, the long stitches must show the boundaries of the forest, the wavy gray stitches are streams and rivers, and here at the top, right under the collar in the small brown stitches is the ravine. Remember Valdi had said, 'Look in your cloaks'!"

Dovid grabbed his own cloak and examined its lining. The peculiar stitching on his was identical to that on mine. He knew I was correct in my discovery but didn't acknowledge it. Instead he asked suspiciously, "What makes you think the small stitching is the ravine?"

"Look," I said, pointing to a segment of one black-trail stitch that crossed the small brown stitching. "There's no reason for part of this trail stitch to cross here unless the small stitching represents the ravine, and that segment of black-trail stitch is the board laid across it!"

My reasoning must have made some sense, because Dovid grudgingly said, "Alright. It's a map made by stitches, so what? How do we know where we are *now*?"

"Well," I said, "I figure this clump of tufted stitches must be the thick woods we came through. If that's so, we're right here on the left bank of the stream, east of the ravine by about sixteen versts. See, the black-thread trail is our route. It is made up of twenty-seven long stitches. They must represent the twenty-seven versts to the border."

In the silence that followed this explanation, I fully enjoyed my moment of cleverness over him.

But soon enough Dovid said, "Well, if we're right on course, my sun theory worked, just like I told you."

"Yes, and the map shows we've made good time too. If it's only sixteen versts to the ravine, we could get to it tomorrow night! That means tomorrow we'd be only three versts from the Austrian Empire. Three versts from Hungary. Three versts from freedom!"

"Then stop your jabbering! Don't just stand there! Get your things! Let's go!" Dovid commanded all at once. We grabbed our cloaks, adjusted our food packs on our backs, and continued through the forest.

We walked for hours, stopping only twice briefly to rest. In the early evening I began to see the truth of

Valdi's warning, for the soil became boggy and the land steep with hills. Our boots and breeches got caked with mud, and our travel grew slower, for we had to slog through wet marshy ground.

Later that night, though, we came to the high ground of a hillock that was barely damp at all. There we covered ourselves with our cloaks and slept until sunrise.

As soon as I woke on that second day, Dovid started giving orders. We weren't to stop at all, he said. Not for meals, not for talk, not for rest, not for prayers.

"We have to stop for prayers," I argued. "We have to say them. It's an affront to God if we don't."

Dovid looked at me as if I were a half-wit. "God's affronted every day. He's used to it."

Shocked that Dovid, as wicked as he was, would forsake our religion, I asked, "Don't you say the prayers? Don't you say the Shema morning and night? Don't you say the daily blessings?"

"I don't say *any* prayers!" he burst out furiously. "Let Reb Svinsky and the rest of Molovsk soak themselves in religious swill. Let them drown in it!"

His face was so twisted that he looked like someone in terrible pain; yet it was his own anger that gave him that appearance.

When he was angry like this—sudden and vicious, I was especially afraid of him; for I sensed that nothing meant anything to him. Nothing at all.

"We won't pray then," I said. "Let's go."

"Praised be Thou, O Lord our God, King of the universe, Maker of light and Creator of darkness, Producer of peace, and Creator of all." As we walked I chanted the morning prayers in my head, making the forest my silent sanctuary. I knew God would hear them, and I felt their power even more for being unspoken.

We had to travel eleven versts that day to reach the border—eight to the ravine and three beyond that to the border itself. Because the land was steep and muddy, it was hard going. We had to cross several brooks, and the water that filled my boots warped them. I threw out the moldy rags stuffed inside them, but still the boots never dried. They were so rough and damp, my feet had sprouted blisters.

We trudged on all day without stopping. I was hungry. My empty stomach growled like a dog. My lips were dry and cracked; and when I ran my tongue over them, they burned right after with a stinging pain. My head throbbed, and my throat felt sore. Worst of all, I was afraid the blisters on my feet had started to bleed.

Then, just about that moment of sundown when the air seems to glow, we came upon it—the ravine. It was an awesome sight, for it was a canyon really, long and deeper than I thought. We walked along it, and in less than ten minutes or so we came to where it narrowed and saw a very skinny board linking one side with the other. I stared at it. This was our crossing.

"Do you think that thing can hold our weight?" I asked, looking uneasily at the rickety plank stretched across the dark deep ravine.

"I guess we'll just have to find out, K'vatsh," Dovid said so indifferently that I wondered whether he was ever afraid of anything. "Don't ask any more stupid questions. Just listen," he ordered. "We're only three versts from the border, but remember the guardhouse is less than six versts south of us. That means there are guards close. *Very* close. There's a chance they won't come this way, but I'm not risking it. We won't cross now. It's too light, and we might be seen. Let's eat in that grove over there and rest. Then just before dark we'll cross the ravine and head straight for the border."

Dovid's reasoning made a lot of sense. We went in among a thick grove of oak trees, and on a crunchy bed of hollow acorn pods we collapsed. First I thought I'd take my shoes off and see how bad my blisters were, but then changed my mind. I didn't want to see. There was no water here to wash them anyway, and I had nothing with which to make bandages. When I'm in Hungary, I told myself, I will take care of them.

For now I took out Aunt Bella's letter and read it. It was an old letter, and most of it was just inquiries about Mama and Papa and myself; yet just reading the words of her New York address and touching the American stamps on the envelope made me feel closer to my goal.

"What's that paper you've got?" Dovid asked.

"It's a letter . . . well, an old letter from my aunt Bella. She lives in New York City, and that's where I'm going. I'm going to live with her and my uncle Yaacov."

"How old is the letter?" Dovid asked slyly.

"About a year and a half . . . maybe a little more."

"Then what makes you think she's still alive?"

"Of course she's alive!" I answered hotly.

"You've no proof she is or isn't," he said. "She could have died of consumption or in childbirth or gotten run down by one of those horse trams they have in big cities."

He was really making me angry now, partly because what he said was true. I *didn't* know for sure whether she was alive or not, yet I was basing my entry into America and my future on the assumption that she was.

"Anyway, your aunt Bella and uncle Whatever have probably moved!" Dovid went on. "They probably live somewhere else now—some other city. And if they moved within New York City, you'd never be able to find them! You'd be as lucky finding a saint in St. Petersburg!"

"I'll just have to take my chances then," I said, thinking this sounded pretty brave. "After all, I'm not turning back."

"Well, good luck," he sneered, "but remember if they're not there anymore, you'll be considered an orphan, and the Americans won't even let you into their fine country! They'll send you right back here."

"I will get in," I said shakily. "I will enter America somehow. I can work there. I'm not afraid of that."

"You?" Dovid hooted. "What can *you* do?"

"I could work in a factory," I said. "Lots of people do that."

"You'd work there day and night until you go blind or become a cripple from it. If I were you, I'd rethink this grand idea of America."

After Dovid said these awful things, he turned his back to me and opened his food pack, but I wasn't going to let him off so easily. "And what are *your* plans?" I asked. "If you don't go to America, where will you go?"

"I'll stay in Hungary," he said. "I can get work there. I'm strong. I can learn the language, and besides," he added with a grin, "I'm good at getting what I want, for I just take it."

"I wish you well," I said, and I took out my food pack too.

This was the last of the food now: a half chunk of cheese, a slice of bread, and one apple. I said my prayers in silence and we ate in silence. A few squirrels ran up and down the trees with acorns in their mouths, and every so often Dovid threw a stone at one, but they were faster than his pitch.

When I finished all the food, I remembered the honey. I drew out the little jar and reached in my pocket for Zalman's knife to pry up the stopper. But the knife was not in my pocket. I stood up and searched my clothes but did not find it. With growing panic I thought back to where I could possibly have left it. I could think of no place. Had it dropped out somewhere as we walked? I frantically checked my pockets again.

"What are you doing?" Dovid asked.

"I'm looking for my knife. I think it's lost!"

"Perhaps it is," he said. "And then . . . perhaps it isn't."

I looked over at him and saw the knife in his hand. He was using it to harpoon his herring.

"How did you get it?" I asked, curious but not surprised by his pickpocketing skill.

He did not answer.

"Well, give it back when you're finished with it," I said.

"Why?" he asked with his mouth full of herring. "It's not *your* knife."

"It is too mine, so give it back."

Dovid held the knife in front of him and examined it closely as if he were some kind of knife expert.

"It doesn't say K'vatsh on it," he said. "It says Zalman."

"Zalman would have wanted me to have it," I cried. "He had to leave before he could take it. I'm keeping it safe for him, so for now it's mine. Give it back!"

"Why should I give it to you?" Dovid asked, as if astounded by my demand. "I need it more than you. I'm the leader. You know that. That's already been decided—or don't you remember?"

The way he said this scared me; yet all my love for Molovsk, for Mama, Papa, and Zalman seemed now connected to that knife, and I wasn't going to give it up.

"You're not a leader," I shouted. "You're a thief! Now give it back!"

"I'll never give it to you," he said, slipping it back into his own pocket. "If you want it, you'll have to come get it," he added dangerously.

I looked at him in outrage. Why was he starting a fight now? Now that we were so close to the border? I hated him. I truly hated him.

"You're a thief," I repeated in a voice filled with rage. "You're a dirty, pig-eating thief! You're a liar, a bully, a rag rat and . . . a . . . a murderer!" I shouldn't have said any of this, for in the next second Dovid picked up a rock and threw it at me. I ducked, and it flew over my head. But he threw another one, and it caught my cheek. Reeling backward, my face exploded in pain; yet after a moment I managed to pick up a rock myself and hurl it at him. I missed and he came after me. But I was fast! I jumped aside and miracle of miracles, as he flew at me, I actually managed to sock him hard in the jaw! That *I* could have done this stunned him, and in his moment of surprise I beat on his shoulder with all my might. My success was short-lived. He wheeled around and started socking me hard in the chest. I was gasping for breath, but he kept on pounding my shoulders and my head. He's going to kill me, I thought. Dovid's cruel enough to do it! I dropped to the ground and he went after me, but I rolled aside and kicked him right in the chin. I heard a crack, and then he let out a horrible animal cry. Had I broken his jaw? I managed to jump up. Our recklessness had gone too far; we had too much at stake now to be fighting.

"Stop!" I cried. "I'm sorry. I really am!" But he wasn't hearing me. He didn't want to hear me. He didn't want to stop. He picked up a thick stick, a branch really, and he quickly broke off the twigs that sprouted from it until all the jagged broken ends protruded menacingly like nails. I couldn't fight that horrible piece of wood. I couldn't! I was so completely terrorized, I had to stop the fighting immediately. "STOP!" I cried. "STOP!"

He ignored my calls and came after me with that deadly stick. I ran, but it was a ridiculous situation. We were enclosed in an oak grove at the side of a ravine, so where could I go? "Stop!" I called again. "Someone might hear us. Please, let's stop this!"

I held up my hands to show him I wanted a truce, and at that instant, exactly that instant, Dovid, like a crazed animal, charged at me and beat me mercilessly. His blows struck me so hard and so fast, it was impossible to defend myself. All I could do was try to cover my head with my arms as the punches came. I don't know how long this terrible beating lasted. It seemed endless to me. At last he stopped as suddenly as he had started; yet I was so hurt in body and in being that for a long time I lay on the ground, sobbing. My clothes were ripped, and my whole body throbbed with pain. Finally, humiliated and bloody, I stood up. Dovid was sitting under an oak tree. He was so calmly eating the last of my honey that, except for his bruised face, he looked as if he'd just had a nice nap.

Dovid is possessed by the Evil Eye, I thought. Truly,

a demon is in him. He looked up at me. "K'vatsh," he smirked, "I warned you once I could beat you up quick and easy, didn't I? Now if you're finished with your woman's weeping, let's cross the ravine."

Hate was too weak a word for what I felt for him then, but I said in a low voice, "I hate you."

"I don't care," Dovid laughed. "Everyone does. Now let's go."

I said nothing more, partly because my mouth hurt so much, but mostly because I didn't want to talk with him again. Ever.

It was twilight now. We had to get across the skinny board at once, while we could still see it. When we came to it, Dovid said, "Now you go first and I'll follow."

I looked at the feeble piece of wood stretched over the black ravine. "Why should I go first? *You're* the leader," I said sarcastically.

"You're going first because you're scrawny," he said. "If the board can't hold you up, it'll never hold me. Besides, if I went first, I might break the board, then how would you get across?"

This was logic to suit only himself. He was using me to test the board for him. But I had no more strength or spirit to argue.

"Cross the board!" he ordered. "Hurry up!"

I moved to the edge of the ravine and looked in. I could not see its bottom, for it was dark as the netherworld. First I tested the board lightly with one foot, then I stepped onto it sideways, moving along it like a river crab. Not daring to look down, I went very, very slowly. I moved one foot out to the side and then steadily brought the other foot up next to it. I heard Dovid's derisive laugh at my method, but it seemed far away, as in a dream. Step, step, step . . . one foot beside the other. A cracking sound! I stopped and stood as if frozen. Another cracking sound! Pay no attention, I told myself. You have to go on. Go on. Go on. Slowly. Go slowly, I repeated silently. Don't look down. One foot beside the other. I shivered. I felt incredibly light, like a fluttering leaf.

How much farther to go? Not much. Ignore Dovid. Ignore him! Keep going. Keep going. The board is sagging! Don't think. One small step at a time. Don't look down! Another side step. That's it. Now another. Almost across! Keep going. The board's creaking louder! Pay no attention. Don't think. Keep going! One step and another and then—I felt it! The familiar feel of soil under my left foot. I brought my right foot to meet it. I had crossed the ravine.

When I turned to look back, I saw in the fading light Dovid stepping out onto the plank. He too tested it with his foot before proceeding, but he did not use my sideways step. He went across it slowly, facing forward. Suddenly a volley of noise cut through the night. GUN-FIRE! I dropped to the ground. Gunshots zinged wildly overhead. Where were they coming from? Where?!

The shooting blasted through the forest, echoing in the chill air. From where I lay I could see Dovid standing about halfway along the plank. He stood still while the sound of bullets exploded all around. He seemed to hesitate.

"Hurry!" I shouted frantically. "Get across!" but then in a second volley of shots, I heard a cry and saw him tumble into the ravine.

20

I lay on the ground trembling, as the gunfire blasted about me. Where are the guards, I thought? Had they seen us? Can they see me? My heart beat so fast I thought it would burst. In terror I stopped my ears with my fingers to lessen the horrifying noise. As I lay in this pitiful way, my mind raced with one idea: If I stand any chance of reaching the border, I must go now! If I hide in the forest tonight, I might evade the guards. But in the light of day they'd spot me easily. And by tomorrow there would be more of them. I have to steal across the border *now*, protected by the shield of night—or not at all.

I glanced at the ravine. Whether Dovid had lost his balance or whether he had been hit by gunfire, I did not know. I knew, though, it was impossible for anyone to climb out of that deep ravine. I was sure of that.

For a moment I considered crawling to the ravine, to

look in and call his name. But what good would that have done? *I* couldn't have gotten him out! And anyway, I reasoned he was probably dead, for he fell a deep, dark way and most likely had a bullet in him. Besides, I thought, were *I* to have fallen in, *he* would have surely gone on. And so, with justification, I left the ravine and ran west.

I stayed low to the ground like an animal, moving swiftly and glancing about for danger, seeing my way between the shadowy shapes of tree trunks. BANG! BANG! BANG! BANG! BANG! The gunshots resounded through the forest like cannon fire. The guards were close to me. I was sure of it! Yet, though I was risking my life by the noise of my running, I figured I was safer as a moving target than a stationary one. How I ran, I do not know, for my feet after walking the whole day were blistered, and my whole body ached from Dovid's beating; yet I ran rabbit-fast, leaping across logs and darting around trees.

I came to a pond and waded through it like a madman, then stumbled westward, tripping from fatigue and the awful pain of my feet. My ears rang with gunfire. Were the soldiers behind me? I mustn't turn around. I had to keep running! Keep running west. What was the name Valdi had given me? Nicki . . . Nickolai. Nickolai what?

I ran on. Once my knee buckled beneath me and I fell into a hole, cutting my leg. I pushed myself out, exhausted and feverish. "Very few succeed in escaping.

Very few succeed in escaping. Very few succeed in escaping . . ." Solomon One-Eye's words echoed horribly in my head. Where are the guards? I wondered. Where *are* they? In my terror I imagined seeing them behind tree trunks or crouched in the bushes. Long branches pointed at me like rifle barrels. From somewhere I was being watched. Eyes were on me! BANG! BANG! BANG! I kept running, running, running.

My breath came hard, my sides hurt, but worst of all as I ran, my brain teemed with memories that flocked and fell over each other like chickens in a feedbin.

Make up any fairy tale you wish.

I'm the leader . . . or don't you remember?

You're a sniveling baby, but I'm almost a man.

Yet remember, ultimately only you *are responsible for yourself.*

Their tears are only water to me.

For it is only when you give that you gain power . . . only then the circle closes.

You can't tell me about stealing and murdering, for I've done both.

I tried to close my mind to the jumbled memories, but it was no use. I couldn't shut them out.

I was so crazed that I didn't know when the gunfire had stopped, yet at some point I was aware that the terrible noise had ended. I slowed down. I had to, for the pain of my feet was very bad.

It was when I slowed down that I first heard the song:

Let's drink a cup to life, my friends,
Let's drink a cup tonight!
For the world is full of strife, my friends,
And tomorrow, we must fight. . . .

I stopped and stood perfectly still. Someone was singing in a slurred voice. Up ahead, beyond the bushes, smoke curled upward. Approaching carefully, I peeked through the shrubbery to see a small clearing in which a man sat on the ground beside a campfire. I could tell immediately he was some sort of guard, for he wore a jacket with the czar's insignia above the pocket. His hat lay beside him, and he was eating a sausage he had cooked over the fire. He was drunk, that was plain. Next to his hat lay an empty brandy bottle, and his eyes had a stupid stare. I heard a noise of leaves moving behind him and saw in the firelight a black horse. I was surprised to see it, for I knew because of the thick woods, the border guards usually worked in foot patrols. But then I remembered what Valdi had said about the lazy scoundrels who swelled the guard ranks, and I grasped the scene at once. He'd taken the horse to have a little drinking party for himself and was now too drunk to get back to the guardhouse. I watched him belch and groan and sing drowsily. For a moment I thought he could see me, for he stopped his singing and looked in my direction, but after a few seconds he began his tedious song again.

I thought gratefully that if I had to come across a guard in the forest, a drunken one was certainly the best kind to encounter. I moved away from him quickly, and as I walked on, the moon rose. It grew brighter and brighter until the whole forest had the gleam of Shabbos silver, and I could see my way easily.

There were no gunshots at all anymore. Not a single one. The only sounds I heard were my own footsteps and the occasional hooting of an owl. In this quiet the land grew steep. As I calmed a little, I longed for rest. I was so weary, I could barely move one foot in front of the other. But at last in great exhaustion I climbed up a sort of crest, and there it was—a little valley cupped like an open hand ready to hold me.

The border! Hungary! I knew it at once, for it was carpeted with crops exactly as Valdi had described. The surprise of seeing it now made my heart explode with joy. I walked to the very edge of the crest. A white shaft of moonlight wrapped about me like a prayer shawl, and in it I gave thanks to the Lord for my deliverance.

Despite my fatigue I was suddenly filled with the energy of happiness. I thought about getting to the farm-house. It was almost midnight now. I could cross the border and rest safely in the bushes for a few hours and begin my search for it at daybreak. I went over the poem Valdi had taught me. I *knew* I could find it!

I sat down at the edge of the crest, just before the shallow sloping of the valley, and for a good while just looked at the land in the moonlight. Ahead of me was hope, and behind me was death. Yet, not fully understanding why, when at last I stood up, I did what I least wanted to do. I turned from the border and began to walk back. Back to the ravine.

21

I cannot say how or why I decided to go back, for it wasn't a decision at all, but a need. Were I to have proceeded across the border, it would have been a straight line to freedom; yet I sensed going back would free me too, though in some different way.

The problem was that I could barely walk now. My whole body cried out for rest. Worst of all, my feet burned as if on fire. Yet I was as determined now to get to the ravine as I had been earlier to leave it. Of course, I was aware that going back was foolhardy. Less than a few hours ago the forest rang with gunfire. Though God had allowed me to escape from that perilous situation once, what right had I to test His mercy again?

But as I went limping back, I shoved all rational thoughts aside and retraced my steps, unthinking as a sleepwalker. I remembered the way, so though I had to go slowly, I went directly. When I got back to the drunken guard he was just as I'd anticipated—asleep. Snoring loudly, he lay on his back with the deep sleep of drink on him. His fire had died down to only a few embers.

I limped up to the guard until I stood right over him. I was so close I noted the white piping on his blue breeches, the brass buckles on his cavalry boots, and above all the long pistol on his belt that in his witless state he hadn't bothered to remove. I glanced behind him and saw his horse, fully saddled and equipped, tied to a tree. I approached it slowly, for I suspected it had the nervous temperament of a fine stallion; and a startled horse, even an old one like Taki, kicks. Nearing the horse cautiously from the left side, I stroked his neck. Unlike Taki, though, he didn't nuzzle his head in my hand, but eyed me suspiciously. I then stroked his silky black mane and whispered to him. I patted his shoulder, and he whinnied. In front of the saddlebag hung a coil of rope that, looped through the halter ring, tied the horse to a tree. I unknotted the rope from the tree and rewound it through the leather loop on the side of the saddle. Then I took the reins from around the pommel and, standing by the horse's shoulder, facing the tail, I put my left foot in the stirrup. With my right hand on the back of the saddle, I used every last bit of energy to push myself up. Then in one motion I swung my right leg over the horse's back and eased down into the saddle. The horse stepped back and neighed in surprise.

Though it frightened me, I held the reins up short as I had often done with Taki. I kept the horse close between my legs and pressed my boots into the short, broad Cossack stirrups. Patting the horse's shoulder, I whispered, "Take me to the ravine."

I only trotted the horse through the forest as there was no trail, and so I had to weave among the trees and across uneven ground. The horse was anxious with his unfamiliar rider, for he chewed nervously on his bit. But I spoke to him all along the way and worked the reins firmly to show him I was now master.

I looked about. The horse gave me a good height for scanning the moonlit woods. But I realized that the height also made *me* more visible.

Retracing my way, in a short while I came to the ravine. I dismounted, and on my knees peered down into the ravine's darkness.

"Dovid!" I called. "Dovid! Dovid!"

But there was no answer. The ravine was silent as a grave.

I tried again, this time a little louder. "Dovid! Dovid, can you hear me? Are you alright?"

I waited for a reply, but none came. I called as loudly as I dared, but again there was no answer. He is dead, I thought, and there is nothing I can do.

I sat there a moment, feeling utterly helpless. But when I stood up to go, I thought I heard a sound. I leaned over the ravine again and called down. A faint, muffled voice rose up from the deep, but I could make out no distinct words. "Dovid! Can you hear me? It's me, Mendel!"

I heard a moan and then in a mumbly way, I heard my name repeated! Then I heard, "Help me."

"I *will* help you," I cried. "I've come back to bring you to the border, but we must act quickly. Are you very hurt?"

"Broken."

"What is broken? Your leg?"

". . . No."

I called again, "What is broken? Tell me."

There was a long pause, then at last one word floated up. "Arm."

"I will get you out," I called.

I uncoiled the rope from the horse's saddle and lowered one end slowly down into the ravine, guiding its destination by Dovid's moaning. By the length of rope I had to lower, I figured the ravine must have been about five meters deep, almost three times his height.

"Do you have the rope now?" I called.

"Yes," he called up weakly.

"Good. Now tie it tightly about your waist, and I will pull you up."

There was no answer.

"Did you hear what I said? Tie it around your waist."

"Can't," he said. "Arm broke."

What can he do? I thought frantically. What? If he

can't tie the rope around himself, there's no way I can get him out!

"You'll have to fasten it somehow," I told him firmly. "There's no other way."

"Can't," he said. His usually angry voice was now pathetic, but I was unaffected.

"Loop it around your belt then. Fasten it somehow— or I will leave."

For some time no more words came up from the ravine, only moans and curses.

"Well?" I called down after a few minutes. "Have you got it tied?"

There was another pause, and then I heard him say, "Yes."

"Is it fastened securely?"

"Yes, lift me up," he whined.

"Give me the knife," I said.

"What?"

"Give me the knife."

"Later."

"Give me the knife now, or you can rot down there until the Messiah comes."

"Can't throw. Arm broke."

"Then use your other arm."

He made no reply, but in a moment Zalman's knife flew up and landed on the ground beside me.

I wiped it off and stuck it in my pocket. "Hold on tight!" I cried. "Hold on to the rope with your good arm and keep your body as straight up as you can!"

I checked that the rope coil was securely fastened to the saddle loop, then I mounted the horse. With a sharp slap on his right flank, he started forward. I went carefully, both looking forward to guide the horse and looking back to the ravine. I made the horse go no more than a few steps at a time, so Dovid wouldn't get bruised coming up. I could hear a lot of moaning but directed the horse onward until at last Dovid's head emerged from the ravine; and then with a few more forward steps of the horse, his whole body was up and out, lying on the ground like a corpse. I tied up the horse and ran to Dovid. The sight was an awful one.

22

Dovid's face shone black with bruises, and his right eye was so swollen it had closed. Above his right ear ran a gash, open and filled with dirt. His cloak and breeches were filthy, and his hair so matted with mud it looked like some dark yarmulke.

I untied the rope he had wound through his belt and he groaned pitiably. I was anxious to leave and could not keep the nervousness out of my voice when I said, "We've got to go! You've got to stand up!"

He groaned once more, and then I had a terrible fear. "Dovid, were you shot?"

"No," he moaned.

I was relieved to hear it, though he was no doubt shamed that his fall was caused by simply losing his balance. With great effort I helped him to his feet; but as I did so, I saw how his right arm hung limp.

I put his good, left arm around my shoulder and

helped him over to the horse. When he saw the splendid stallion tied to the oak tree, his face lit up with surprise.

"How . . . ?" he began, but I cut him off. "I'll tell you later—we don't have time."

Somehow I had to get Dovid with his broken arm mounted on the horse. At first I thought he could push off with his left foot into my hands, hold the pommel with his left hand, and swing himself over. But after trying this a few times, I saw he didn't have the strength to accomplish it. Besides, the strange flurry of legs and arms was making the horse paw the ground with agitation. Then I hit upon it! Close by stood an oak stump, about a meter high. I helped Dovid over to it. With a good deal of pushing and pulling, I got him on the stump. "Stand up!" I ordered. He did so, and I brought the horse around. Now it was much easier for him to slide into the saddle, and so while I kept the horse steady and encouraged him, Dovid mounted the stallion, and we took off.

Because Dovid had little strength, I was afraid he'd fall. To prevent this I told him to hold tightly around my waist with his good arm. In this way we went through the forest, not trotting now, but cantering to gain a smoother ride for Dovid, as well as to gain speed. I was very nervous. I had no idea if there were guards in the forest or not. I felt the vulnerability of being discovered with a stolen horse, and I felt the burden of traveling with Dovid. I carefully thought over what we must do and told the plan aloud to him.

"First, we must return the horse," I said. "It belongs to a soldier, but he's asleep. Then we must get to the border, only about a verst past him. We'll cross into Hungary and look for the farmhouse. If we're lucky . . . and you can walk it, we can get there." Dovid gave a sort of grunt, which I took for approval, and we went on.

As before, I tried to see in the dim forest as we rode, looking about for danger. I could see nothing—only dark shadows; yet very suddenly the horse stopped and refused to move. I knew horses did this when they were frightened by something unexpected, for I had often seen Taki stop short at the abrupt sight of a rabbit. I listened and heard nothing. I looked around but still saw only shadows. Yet I too sensed danger, as someone might at the sudden pause of birdsong.

The horse would not go. I couldn't force him ahead, so I turned him to the left, hoping this movement would lessen his alarm. He went a few steps and stopped again; he would not move.

"Kick him," said Dovid.

"That doesn't help," I said. "He just refuses to go forward."

I looked about again. Was I imagining or was I really seeing some movement in the bushes?

"Let's go," Dovid mumbled wearily.

"Shaah! Don't talk!" I felt a bone-chilling fear. The horse whinnied.

"HALT IN THE NAME OF THE CZAR!" Two

guards sprang from the bushes, rifles pointed directly at us, triggers cocked! "HALT!"

The two men, young and tall, ran toward us. One of the guards stood a bit away with his rifle pointed at us, while the other ran up to the left side of the horse. "Where did you get that horse?" he demanded. I looked into his dark eyes, and they told me he already knew the answer.

"I took it," I answered. "I had to. My brother and I were camping in the woods so we could catch some fish this morning, but my brother fell into a hole, broke his arm, and couldn't get out. So I borrowed the horse to pull him out. It belongs to a man up ahead who was sleeping. I was just returning it. That's the truth."

The guard's face was not cruel, but cold. He listened to this lie for what it was. "Show me your Governor's Permit," he commanded as he quickly lit a small paraffin candle.

Dovid's arm was still around my waist, and I could feel his trembling, which, surprisingly, was just as strong as my own. I reached into the pocket of my breeches and pulled out the now very wrinkled permit Valdi had given me. As the guard examined it in the flickering light, I kept my face down so he couldn't see on it the terror I felt.

"Name?" he asked.

"As it says there, sir, Nickolai Nickolovitch."

He looked over the forged paper skeptically.

"Where's *your* identification?" he suddenly asked Dovid.

"I lost mine, sir," Dovid answered weakly. "When I fell, all my things fell out into the dark hole. My name is Dmitri Nickolovitch."

"We live at a farm," I broke in, "not far from here. We were camping yesterday afternoon when the accident happened. I didn't want to leave my brother down there, so I took the horse, but . . ."

"You're lying," the man interrupted, and the matter-of-fact way he said it made further lies useless. I said nothing more to bolster my story, nothing more to defend us. I glanced around. I didn't see any horses. The guards had probably been combing this area on foot, looking for smugglers. As if reading my thoughts, the guard blew out the candle and said, "I've seen too many of your kind to believe you. Though I must say, you're a good deal younger than most. I don't know what you're running from—maybe a father who beat you . . . but I don't think so. At first I thought you were gypsies, but now, the way you talk with that absurd accent makes me think you're Jews, probably runaway Cantonists. We keep watch over this border and have been finding all kinds of criminals. Only a few hours ago a man was found trying to escape, but we stalked him on foot. You must have heard the guns. He escaped alright—escaped this world forever! Now get off that stolen horse. You'll be walked back to the guardhouse, and you can tell your lie to the captain."

I looked at this guard and the one who now had put his rifle down and was urinating in the bushes. "We will go with you humbly, sir, and explain the truth of what I said, for we are innocent of crime. But please, before anything, by the mercy of the saints give my brother some water, for as you see he is in a bad way. Saint Nicholas bless you, sir."

The guard darted a quick glance at Dovid, who, it must be said, looked frightful. He opened his metal canteen and handed it to Dovid, but I intercepted it. "His arm's broken, sir. I'll have to hold it for him." I turned around in the saddle and held the canteen near Dovid's mouth. Dovid looked at me, puzzled, but my eyes told him to take a drink and he did. When he'd finished, I held the canteen out to the man; but just as he reached for it, I swung it sharply up so that the canteen struck him hard under the chin, and the cold water splashed into his face while in the same moment I kicked my heels with a fury into the horse's flanks. We were off! We galloped through the woods as if on a creature possessed. I heard the delayed rifle shots aimed at our backs but knew that we had a horse and so the advantage.

"HOLD ON!" I shouted to Dovid. "HOLD TIGHT!" The horse, frightened witless, galloped dangerously over the dark uneven land, but I, just as frightened, made no attempt to slow him. It seemed only moments when we came to the steep rising terrain. "LEAN FORWARD!" I yelled to Dovid as I knew that to scale it, the horse would need some weight taken off his hindquarters. When we reached the crest, I pulled up on the reins to slow the horse down and gradually brought him to a stop.

"This is the border," I told Dovid, my voice breaking with emotion. "Down there is Hungary. Down there somewhere is the farmhouse."

"Are you sure?" Dovid asked.

"Yes, it's just as Valdi had described it to me. I was here earlier tonight and when I saw it, I knew it."

"You were *here*, at the border?" Dovid asked in amazement. "Why didn't you go on?"

"I had to close a circle," I answered.

"I don't understand."

"I don't completely understand either," I said.

Then, so the horse wouldn't trip, I held his head well up with the reins, and we rode down into the valley.

23

Right of road
Left of lake
Past three farms
Dirt path take.

Before the sheep
Beyond the stable
Where holes are hearts
Beneath a gable.

I repeated the poem in my head and tried to remember everything Valdi had told me. The problem was I was so weary, I could not think clearly. And Dovid was no help at all. He began to moan a lot, and when we rode over a rocky part of the land, he cried out in suffering. He was getting weaker, and I prayed we'd reach the farmhouse soon.

Every so often as we rode, I heard the echoes of gunfire, but they were only in my mind. I knew the guards could not have followed us. Bang! Bang! Bang! It was like tiny explosions in my head that came suddenly and then faded again.

The valley was about seven versts from the crest to the flatland. I slowed the horse to a walk, for it was tired, and, besides, at our fast pace Dovid had nearly fallen off. By the time we reached the floor of the valley, it was dawn. All about us the night-gray crops grew slowly green. We came to a pond where I let the horse drink and thought over where we must go. I was at the right of a road, but surely, I thought, this pond could not be called a lake? I decided to ride on to see if there was a real lake up ahead.

Soon we did come to a lake, not a large one, but certainly bigger than the pond. I turned down the path left of it, and we passed three large farms, each set among beech trees about one verst from each other. There was only one dirt path, off to the right, and I followed it for about a quarter verst. When I saw the small stable and beyond it a pasture of grazing sheep, my heart leapt. There was a chicken coop and, between, a wood farmhouse of two stories with gabled windows and shutters carved with hearts.

We rode into the yard, and I dismounted. Then I helped Dovid down, and he nearly fell on top of me in the process, as he was so weak. He remained on the ground while I looked around. The sun was full up now.

I could hear the bleating of sheep and the squawking of chickens, and their noise mingled with the faint gun sounds in my head.

I walked toward the house and saw smoke puffing out of its chimney. Suddenly a door banged open and two blond children, a boy and a girl, ran out with much noise. They each carried a tiny, straw-filled basket. The children were no more than five years old. They looked so much the same in height and weight I thought them twins.

When they caught sight of me, they stopped in terror, as if they saw the Evil Eye. Shrieking in their Hungarian language, they ran back in the house. After a moment, though, they came back out, following in fearful curiosity a tall blond man with neither beard nor moustache.

I must have looked a sight, as the man himself seemed startled by my appearance. He spoke to me roughly in his language. Then, seeing I had as much understanding of his words as a dog, he tried Russian. "Who are you?" he asked. "What do you want here?" The man's face was hard and his tone unfriendly.

I didn't trust him enough to tell him my story, and yet this was certainly the man Valdi had told me about. I knew no one else in the world to help me, so I said, "Please sir, I'm very tired and hungry. And my friend is sick."

The man looked to where I pointed and then went quickly over to Dovid. He knelt over him with a grave face. Then he stood up and without saying a word went back into the house. In a minute he came out again, followed by a tall, lean boy of about eighteen. He gave the boy the horse to stable and other instructions I couldn't understand. When this was done, the man turned back to me and said, "You will stay here."

He said this without warmth and without the slightest hospitality; yet I was glad. I looked over at the farm-house, and I thought of crackling fires, cooked meals, and warm blankets. I began to follow him toward the house.

"STOP!" the man shouted to me, as one might shout to a robber. "STAY!"

I froze where I was, and he walked quickly into the house again. Completely confused now, I went to sit by Dovid, who in his pain lay on the ground. I don't know how long I sat in the farmyard, but it seemed a long while. At last the man came out again carrying a large tin tub filled with steaming water. Placing the tub in the corner of the yard, he beckoned for me to come to him. "Wash," he commanded.

I was embarrassed at the idea of bathing in an open yard; yet I took off my clothes at the man's insistence. I stepped into the hot water, and at once my blisters burned as if on fire. I cried out, but he showed no mercy. He began to scrub me with a white soap that was prob-ably made with pig fat and a brush like a small porcupine. Despite my hollering, he seemed most concerned about my hair; he washed it three times with a dark, foul-smelling powder, rinsing it each time with a pitcher of water.

When I'd dried myself, he put a sort of medicine on my blisters, bandaged them, and told me to dress in the clean clothes he had brought. I did this while he emptied the water into the bushes and went back into the house.

By the time I was dressed in these clothes that were much too big, he'd returned with a fresh tub of hot water in which I saw now he was going to torture Dovid in the same way. "Watch his right arm," I said, "it's broken."

But the man, lifting Dovid easily, was gentle with him.

"Go in the house," he shouted at me. "Mother Matya will give you food."

I walked toward the house and passed through a doorway painted gaily with flowers. I opened the door and though I stepped into a kitchen, I felt I had entered heaven. In the center of the kitchen stood a large, half-open hearth made of green tiles, in which a small fire crackled. Above the tiles were hung copper pots that sparkled in the firelight and above them, two rows of old jugs painted in all the colors of the rainbow. All about me the plaster walls were white as snow. On the high part they were trimmed with painted plates and on the low part covered with colorful embroideries. In one corner stood a carved and gaily painted spinning wheel. In the center of the kitchen stood a large table spread with a richly embroidered cloth and laden with food. I stared at everything on it: the earthen bowls of cheese and butter, the big blue pitcher of cream, the little mountains of purple grapes and rosy apples, the oval bread still steaming from the oven, and, best of all, the honey cake in the shape of a bear!

As I stood staring, an old woman entered, and she was as decorated as everything else. She was very aged, for her skin was thin and slightly yellowed, like the pages of an old prayer book; yet her bell-shaped skirt and pointy little boots were cherry red. She wore a black apron stitched with red flowers, and her gray hair was topped by a small black cap embroidered with white snowflakes.

She said something to me in Hungarian that I didn't understand. Then she smiled, gesturing for me to sit at the table. When I did, she brought me a plate and piled it with all the delights. Next she went to the copper *samovar* and poured me a glass of tea, in which she stirred a spoonful of jam. All the while she chattered at me in a very friendly way, not at all bothered by whether I understood her or not.

I ate a small slice of bread, but though I hadn't eaten in a long time, I could not eat more. I sipped the tea and while I did, the door banged open and the man came in. After a few words with the old woman, he sat down across from me.

"I have put your friend in a back room," he said. "And

I have sent Gyori to fetch a doctor. He will rest in the back now, and Mother Matya will bring his food on a tray."

"Thank you," I said.

The old woman brought the man a glass of tea. He drank and spread his bread with a great mound of cheese. Then he leaned across the table and stared into my face. "Who are you?" he asked. "Where are you from?"

I looked up into his eyes. "I am a Jew," I answered boldly; and as he did not seem disturbed by this, I told him my story. I told him about Molovsk, about Valdi, about Dovid, about the ravine. I must have left much out, though, as I was nearly too exhausted to talk. As I spoke, he ate. I had no idea what effect my words had on him, for his face showed no emotion, nor did he make any comment. I paused often in my tale, for the gun sounds were in my head, and the kitchen walls seemed to billow like curtains.

When I finished, he said nothing. He seemed neither surprised nor moved by anything I'd said. At last he leaned across the table, looked into my eyes, and asked, "Where did you get the horse?"

"I stole it from a drunken Russian," I answered.

He smiled for the first time and said, "Well done!"

The kitchen door burst open, and the two children ran in. They stood by the table to stare at me. The old woman spoke to them gently, then she spoke to the man. After a moment he turned to me.

"My name is Sandor and this is my mother, Mother Matya. She tells me you need to rest, and she is right. Go with her now. Rest. You have told your story, but not your dream. Tomorrow you will tell me your dream."

24

I fell into a sleep so deep that the sun set, rose, set, and rose again before I woke. When I did wake, it was to a small rolling sound. I jumped down from the bed and opened the door. The little boy was playing with a brightly colored toy cart. Rag people, no bigger than his fingers, rode in the cart as he rolled it back and forth over the wood floor. When he saw me, he picked up the cart and thrust it into my hands. I did not know toys could be so beautiful—so pretty and elaborately carved. When I stroked its smooth wood, there came a sweet memory of holding Zalman's boat. The boy stared up at me and asked for his cart back, and suddenly the sweet memory vanished, and the cart in my hands felt like a distant thing. I handed it back and closed the door.

After washing and praying, I got dressed, then walked about the house. It was a large farmhouse. In back of the kitchen were three rooms. As the doors to these rooms were open, I peeked in. Like the one I had slept in, they were all bright with embroidered pillows and wool coverlets. Dovid was in none of them.

In the kitchen Mother Matya was stirring porridge on the fire. When she saw me, she bade me sit at the table as before and served me the porridge with tea. I ate hungrily. She gave me a great chunk of milk cheese with rye bread and a wedge of honey cake, which I ate with a pile of peach preserves. And it was curious, for there was no pork on the table as is the custom for peasant breakfasts.

When I'd finished, I walked outside. It was a beautiful summer morning. All about, the gray-green leaves of the beech trees rippled in the breeze. I walked toward the pastures beyond the farmhouse. They were yellowing with the season and dotted with sheep. I caught sight of Sandor and Gyori far away in the fields. Sandor saw me too and came to me.

"Mother Matya says if you sleep through a whole day in this life, you get an extra day in heaven."

"I guess I did sleep pretty long."

"You needed it," he said. He must have been right too, for the gun sounds were no longer in my head.

"Where's Dovid?" I asked.

"I have work to do. Follow me, and I will tell you."

I followed him out into the fields. He and Gyori pumped water into buckets and then filled the stone troughs. They set out big blocks of salt about the pasture for the sheep and with shovels turned the dung down into the earth. When all this was done, Sandor sat on a bench under a tall beech tree and from a long hunk of wood, set to carving. I sat beside him, and while he carved, he spoke to me.

"I have sent Dovid away to my cousin Arpad who can nurse animals and people both. He will set Dovid's arm and care for him. It will take a few weeks."

I thanked him for his help but had an uneasy feeling he was not telling me the truth. We sat together in silence for several moments, then Sandor spoke again.

"So, Mendel, what is your dream?"

"What do you mean?" I asked.

"The dream that's in you. Unseen, like the ladle that's in this piece of wood. The ladle's there, and I just help bring it out. People are like uncarved wood. They hold a dream inside them others can't see. What is *your* dream?"

"To go to America," I said.

He looked surprised. "How do you plan to get there?"

"On a ship from Hamburg, Germany."

"Where's your ticket?"

"I have no ticket," I replied. "I will buy one in Hamburg."

"Where will you get the money for this ticket?"

"I have one hundred rubles."

"And tell me, Mendel, what good are rubles in Germany?" I hadn't thought of this problem, but before I could tackle it, Sandor asked, "What will you use for a passport?"

"Do I need a passport to leave?" I asked.

"Of course you do!" he said impatiently. "And where do you want to go in America?"

"To my aunt Bella," I stammered. "My mother's sister who lives in New York City."

"When did you last hear from her?"

"A year and a half ago," I answered, annoyed by all his questions. Though this man had housed me for two nights, I didn't owe him so much information—rather I thought he owed me some.

Sandor carefully pared a long strip off his wood and let the curl fall to the ground. "My judgment is that your dream is unwise," he said sternly. "Too risky."

His words and his tone made me angry. Without thinking I said, "What do I care about the judgment of a liar!"

Taken aback at my outburst, he asked, "What do you mean?"

"Dovid!" I exclaimed. "After we arrived, you told me he was resting in a back room; yet I don't believe he stayed here at all! You lied to me!"

Sandor looked at me in surprise, and despite my mounting fear, I continued rashly, "And why did you send him away to your cousin? If you were concerned about him, why didn't you ask Gyori to fetch a doctor?"

Sandor looked straight into my eyes and said firmly, "I sent him away only to protect us all. I didn't want any more trouble. I mean no harm to you or to Dovid, but it is dangerous for me to have two Russian runaways here. One I could possibly explain. But *two* such boys suddenly appearing would start the neighbors talking, and I don't want to be suspected. That's why I didn't get a doctor. I assure you, though, my cousin Arpad can take care of Dovid's arm. He can set it as well as any doctor. I am telling you the truth."

The direct way he spoke made me regret I had accused him of lying. "I am sorry," I said.

As acceptance of my apology, Sandor simply nodded and peeled another long strip off his wood.

"What did you mean when you said you didn't want any *more* trouble?" I asked. "What kind of trouble did you make before?"

Sandor gave a scornful smile and simply said, "I have not made trouble. I have been accused of making trouble."

"Why?"

"I am only a Hungarian who loves being free. You know we are ruled by the Austrian Emperor, Franz Josef, and his Hapsburg noblemen. None of them care a turnip about us. But we want our freedom. We want an independent Hungary with Hungarian rulers, not Austrian puppets. We want a new Hungarian state with full rights for all. My wife too wanted this. She was a Jew and saw how this emperor took away the rights for which the Jews here had fought so hard. The right to establish schools, to lease lands, to take up a profession, and to live in the cities. My wife and I joined with other Hungarians, Jews and gentiles, who wanted change. We were so strong that for a while even the nobility in Vienna listened to us and gave us much that we demanded. But less than a year later the Austrians changed their minds. The Emperor, afraid we'd topple his throne, sent his army to defeat us. Your Czar Nicholas sent his army to help him! This whole countryside swarmed with Russian soldiers, and they killed people like flies. I was suspected of spying—put in jail, but released after the Russians left. I was lucky, for they thought me too unimportant to worry about. When I got out, I saw our brief independence was snatched away. At this time my wife gave birth to little Eva and Lajos. She died in childbirth."

Sandor pared the end of the wood in quick, even movements. He kept his eyes fixed on his work. "It is perhaps best that she did not live to see how the Hungarian ox is now under the yoke of Austria—tighter than ever."

"Do you still fight for freedom?" I asked.

"From the Tisza River to the German border, I work with others. In October I will go to Belden, a town west of Salzburg, where we will draft a proclamation of freedom. Danger or not, we will not give up; for one day not just Hungary, but all Europe, will be free."

"But aren't you afraid of being caught again?" I asked.

"I am not afraid. Besides, I'm clever. Still, I must be careful. Informers are everywhere. Although we have informers informing us about the informers! Your 'Valdi' is one of these. He is both crazy and cunning. His real name is not Valdi, of course, for he has several names. He has set up a web of spies and freedom fighters across the Russian border, Romania, and into Hungary. He has a cat's cunning, but he took a risk sending children to me. And not only *Russian* children but *Jewish* as well! The whole business endangers himself and me too."

"Why didn't you turn us away then?" I asked.

"I wanted to. But you boys were as pitiful as stray dogs, and I try to help anyone seeking freedom from czarist and Hapsburg rule. Though," he added wryly, "I don't normally bathe and feed children."

"If I'm a danger to you now, I will leave," I said.

"You cannot go," he replied.

"Why not?"

"Because though you've been lucky so far, your luck will run out in Hungary. Jews are no more loved here than in Russia, and you, Mendel, are a Jewish boy traveling with neither kin, country, nor coin."

"But I must go. There's nothing else I can do."

"Don't talk foolish!" he snapped. "There is much you can do. You can work here on my farm. I would say you're a relative who has come to work with me. Or, if you prefer, I could take you to live with the Jews in Debrecen or even Budapest. There are many kind families who would take you in. You could live in safety."

"It's not my dream to live in safety!" I protested. "It's my dream to live in freedom." Then I added, "Same dream as yours."

Sandor stared at me, and his blue eyes reflected a fear.

"I am an adult and can take care of myself," he said with emotion. "You are still a boy and so need protection!"

Aggravated by this discussion, he brushed his blond hair from his forehead, resumed his carving, and said nothing more. He was right. I had no means of getting to Hamburg, let alone on a ship to America; yet I didn't want to give up . . . not yet.

The morning breeze suddenly blew stronger, making the boughs above us sway and the leaves tremble noisily. Using the flat side of the blade like a file, Sandor skimmed his wood lightly again and again to smooth it.

"You could help me," I said to him at last.

"I have just offered you my help, and you didn't want it."

"You could take me with you to Salzburg."

"Impossible!"

"Why? Away from your neighbors, no one will know or care who I am!"

"No!"

"I would be no trouble to you. I ask for no money, just the protection of traveling with you."

He turned to me. "Don't you see?" he said. "I don't approve of you going. I think you're wrong to try to get to America on your own. It's unsafe. It won't work!"

"I'll make it work," I said.

"Mendel, you're too stubborn for your own good."

"If I weren't stubborn, I wouldn't be *here*!"

"Luck and pluck," Sandor answered. "That combination gets you only so far."

I thought about this for a moment, then said carefully, "If you took me to Salzburg, that's more than half the way to Hamburg. And if we arrive there safely, half the danger would already be behind me."

Suddenly Sandor stabbed his knife hard into the bench. "Boy tricks!" he cried. "I thought I was whittling down this wood here; yet all the while *I'm* the one that's been whittled down—by you!"

"Are you saying you'll take me?" I asked.

"Yes, I will take you, but we don't go until October. That's nine weeks. When we leave, Dovid can come here and work. But while you're here, you must be Nickolai Nickolovitch. If anyone asks, I will say you're a relative who was sent to help me. And you will help too. In the weeks ahead Gyori and I must clean the barns for winter, repair the fences, and harvest the feed crops. You'll do your day's work, same as us."

So for the next nine weeks I worked on Sandor's farm. To his neighbors, the eggseller and the woolman who came to call, I was Nickolai, a nephew, one of two sons of an older sister who had married a Ukrainian tanner and now lived in Kiev. "When Nicki leaves," Sandor told them, "it will be his brother Dmitri's turn to visit." Sandor informed everyone that I was a city boy to whom nine weeks of farm life were a tonic. And the truth hid in this lie, for they were. Each day I woke at the rooster's crow and after breakfast began my chores. Sandor owned a hundred head of sheep, which he kept in three pastures. Year after year he moved the animals from one pasture to another, so that manured pastureland of alfalfa and clover would in the next season grow the corn feed. Now, before autumn, we had to harvest the corn, store it in the barn, and move the animals down to the newly harvested field so they could graze on the corn stubble.

I plucked the weeds out of the alfalfa, picked the beech nuts from the trees, filled the water troughs, and fed and groomed the soldier's horse, which was now Sandor's. I learned many things on the farm, including how to right an upturned sheep without hurting it, how to give orders to a sheepdog, how to tell timothy grass from clover and how to recognize the bleat of a sheep in distress.

Best of all, I learned some carving as I sat with Sandor in the late afternoons while he made what he called "sheep jewelry." Sandor hated putting bells on his sheep. "Bells are worse than bees for agitating a flock," he said. Instead, he carved round wooden trinkets that hung from their collars. For each ewe he'd make a large trinket with some object carved on it such as a horse-shoe, a pot, or a hammer. And for the ewe's lamb, the same carving, only on a smaller trinket. In this way he could easily tell the parentage of all his sheep. Using Zalman's knife, I made two trinkets carved with a little boat, which Sandor swore he would use in the spring.

When the Jewish Holy Days came, Sandor said we'd all rest from work, and pray, each in our own way. It was a new year for me, and Sandor said it would bring a new beginning. I thought so too; for though I couldn't see it yet, I felt something good lay ahead. Like day, that while you sleep, waits on the other side of the world.

Then one cool October afternoon it was time to leave.

Into a small willow basket Mother Matya packed bread, cabbage salad, and cheese for our trip. She gave me a tender parting hug that for a moment brought my own dear mother to mind. Just then a small droshky pulled into the farmyard. Whooping with joy, Eva and Lajos ran to meet it.

I took the basket and the little sack of clothes Sandor had given me and went outside. Dovid climbed down from the driver's ledge. Sandor, who was speaking with his cousin, called to me. "Arpad will take us as far as Karcag, but we must leave now."

I looked at Dovid. He had gained weight, and his face was smooth and browned from the sun. The way he picked up his bag and swung it over his shoulder was proof his arm was healed. In that rushed, odd moment of his coming and my going, I went up to him and said, "Your arm's good as before."

"Just about," he replied.

"I'm going to Hamburg," I told him. "Sandor is taking me to Salzburg."

Dovid said nothing to this, so I said, "You will like it on Sandor's farm. There's much that's good here."

Again he said nothing, so I simply said, "Good-bye."

"Good-bye, Mendel," he said with indifference, yet not calling me K'vatsh, as before.

I turned from him, gave Lajos and Eva hugs, then climbed into the droshky. It rolled out of the farmyard. Through its little square window, I saw Dovid suddenly put down his bag to wave to me. I waved back, but he'd already turned away.

25

For two weeks Sandor and I bumped along the roads to Salzburg. In public coaches and hired droshkies we crossed valleys in the first week and rounded mountain crests in the second. I did not like sitting inside a coach, for it was difficult to see; and when it held other passengers, I had to play the part of a simple boy to ward off questions. So whenever he could, Sandor arranged to sit up on the driver's ledge with me next to him. I loved traveling this way. From the ledge I could survey the land as far as fifty versts. In the morning I could spot eagles and falcons, and in the evening, wild deer and boar.

At night we'd stop at inns and eat heartily. Sandor, having adopted some of his wife's customs, did not eat pork, so the two of us would share a lake fish or a cabbage and dumpling stew. He paid for all the food, and when I offered him my rubles, he'd cry, "Don't be foolish!"

At the end of the second week, we traveled up the long Alpine road to Salzburg. As soon as we arrived, Sandor took me to an inn. "Give me all your rubles now," he commanded. "I have business to do and will return tonight." Without questioning him, I gave him all my money.

Throughout that day I amused myself by climbing the narrow streets and looking into shop windows. I marveled that I could understand some of the German spoken here, as many words were the same as in Yiddish.

Night fell, and Sandor did not come back. In the little room of the inn, I lay on my bed, fully clothed. Often when I thought I heard footsteps, I'd spring to the window and search the dim streets. But the night hours rolled slowly as the wheels of an ox cart, and Sandor did not return.

Was he in trouble? Had he been caught working against the Austrian Empire? Was he hurt? My mind danced with fearful thoughts. Over the dark city a chorus of churchbells sluggishly tolled the hours. Then, so late at night that it was early in the morning, the door opened, and Sandor walked in. "You're still awake!" he cried. He lit the oil lamp and thrust into my hands a bread roll stuffed with cheese, which I ate hungrily.

Then he sat next to me on the bed and drew wonders from his coat. "Do I need a passport?" Sandor asked in a mocking tone, mimicking the question I had asked him weeks ago. "Yes!" he declared. "And now you have it!" He handed me a small brown book with the czar's emblem on the cover. I opened it and found my real name written inside, "Mendel Cholinsky." My own passport. Before I had time to understand this surprise, he said, "I have gone to great trouble to get you this 'passport.' As soon as you arrive at the port in Hamburg, you must get it stamped with an exit visa. Without delay. Once it is stamped by the Germans, the Americans will believe it is real."

"Isn't the passport real?" I asked.

"It's as real a Russian passport as *you'll* ever have!" he answered. Then, changing the subject he said, "Now look what magic trick I performed today. I turned your Russian rubles into gold." Sandor dug something out of his pocket and put it into my hand.

"You bought me a ticket!"

"Yes, you'll leave on the fourth of November, on the *Hamburg Queen*."

"Fourth of November—that's less than three weeks! Oh, you're very kind to do this for me!" I exclaimed, now wide awake with excitement.

"I'm not kind; I'm clever. Now, look, here are fifty *deutsche marks* for you. That's German money. You'll need these for your travel to Hamburg and for the food you must take with you on the ship." Sandor put the marks into a leather pouch with a strap and hung it around my neck. "Tuck the pouch under your shirt, and whatever you do, don't count the money in public!"

I patted the little pouch bulging with coins. I held the passport in my hands, moving my fingers over the grainy feel of its leather cover. I gazed at the ticket as if it were an illusion.

I was overwhelmed by all this, yet I asked for something more, telling him what had been a nibbling mouse at my heart. "I fear my parents are worrying," I said. "It's been almost three months since I left Molovsk, and they don't know where I am, or even if I'm alive! I must write them to let them know I'm well and that I am really going to America!"

Sandor's face looked grave. "You cannot do that," he said. "Writing to your parents now might endanger them. Wait. Wait until you're safe in America two or three months, then contact them. Have your aunt write them a letter and put your letter inside hers. Now think nothing more of your parents, Mendel. Tomorrow you will begin your journey from here to Nürnberg, in Germany. I've made the arrangements."

The next afternoon Sandor and I walked along the bank of the Salzach River to the livery stable. There he introduced me to a man named Emil who would take me and six other passengers across the German border, then through Munich to Nürnberg. Filled with nervous excitement, I chattered and checked my pockets again and again for my passport, money, ticket, letter, knife, and the map Sandor had made, showing the towns I'd pass in Germany.

As much as I talked, Sandor was quiet. Then when Emil announced he was about to leave, Sandor pressed something into my hand. "Take this," he said.

It was a wooden knife case, polished smooth as stone and with a little sheep carved into it. The case was the perfect size for Zalman's knife, and I loved it at once.

"*Köszönöm*," I said in Hungarian. "Thank you for everything."

From Salzburg to Hamburg was nearly a thousand versts; yet it was an easy journey, for with a passport I could use my own name and had no need to hide that I was a Jew. After Nürnberg I changed coaches several times, stopping at night in simple lodgings with the drivers. Near Nordhausen it began to rain, and we were delayed two days because of the slow pace we had to take on the muddy roads. Then, midday on the third of November, I arrived in Hamburg. From the horse tram that took sea travelers south to the port, I caught glimpses of wide green parks and large brick houses. We passed several carriages pulled by horses with flowers on their manes and their tails braided like Shabbos bread. Everything I saw looked rich. If things are this grand in Germany, I thought, how much grander yet they'll be in America.

The tram turned, and suddenly I had a brief glimpse of water. The port! I strained to see where the boats were, but from the tram I could see only buildings. When I got down from the tram, I wanted to explore the docks along the estuary right then; but I remembered Sandor's warning to get my exit visa without delay, and so I made my way toward the long, low building. German officers in gray uniforms stood at the entrance shouting orders, which very few of the travelers seemed to understand. I pushed my way through the crowds, keeping an eye out for pickpockets. Soon I found myself inside the large emigration hall. There was a line of bearded men in frock coats, and women wearing wigs and wrapped in shawls. "Juden," the sign above them read. This was the Jewish line, and I fell in behind them. The wait was hopelessly long. From what I could see, several German customs officers and ship representatives sat behind a long table filling out forms and asking questions. Endless questions.

It seemed that right answers were of the highest importance. Arguments broke out over them, and once I saw a woman weep when, because of a wrong answer, her whole family was turned away. I too could win or lose, I thought. I must think before answering! As I waited, I went over all the traplike questions they might ask and the tricky ways I'd slip out of them.

The gas lamps were lit by the time it was my turn. I stood before six men at a long table. One of them barked questions at me in German. When I had difficulty understanding, he spoke in a bad Yiddish to me.

"Name?"

"Mendel Cholinsky."

"Nationality?"

"Russian."

"Race?"

"Jewish."

"Age?"

"Twelve."

"Relative in America?"

"My aunt Bella, sir."

"What is her address?"

I pulled the now much tattered letter out of my pocket. And the man took it with a grimace, as if I'd handed him a dead mouse. He copied the return address into his book.

"Shifskarten?"

"Sir?"

"Ticket, do you have a ticket or not?"

"Yes, sir," I stammered, fumbling in my pocket.

"While you're rooting around in there, dig up your passport as well."

I handed him my ticket, which he glanced at briefly, but he inspected the passport for what seemed a long while. As he looked at it, it occurred to me that the passport might be forged. How, in fact, did Sandor get hold of such a rare thing? Either he bribed to get a real one, or he bribed to get a fake one. The sudden realization of my ignorance of the matter made me feel a growing terror.

"Why are you thin?" he suddenly asked.

"I've always been thin," I answered. "It's just the way I am."

"And you don't look like a Jew."

"I am," I said.

The man looked at me, thought for a moment, then said, "I am stamping your passport with an exit visa, but attaching a note that it is provisional on obtaining another stamp you'll receive if you pass the shipping company's health examination." Then pointing to the far corner of the hall, he added, "Tomorrow, you line up for the examination over there."

"But, sir," I said, my voice cracking, "my ticket is for the boat that leaves *tomorrow*. I must be on it!"

But without looking up, all he said was, "Next!"

26

I paid five marks that night to sleep in one of the large men's dormitories that lined the waterfront. I hardly slept, for even though I put my money under my pillow, I was afraid of getting it stolen in such a place. Besides, the spitting, snoring, and laughing of the more than one hundred men and boys would have kept even the dead awake.

As soon as it was morning, I ran to stand in the line for the medical inspection. In groups of twenty we were let into a large room. This room was steamy, and the floors and walls completely made of white tiles. A sickly looking young man who worked for the shipping line gestured for me to come to him.

"There's a note attached to your passport that your ship leaves today! Why didn't you get inspected last week?"

"I only arrived in Hamburg yesterday," I answered.

"Where are your parents?" he demanded.

"I am traveling alone."

"Why are you not dressed as a Jew?"

"My parents are freethinkers."

"What is the amount of your travel money?"

"Forty-five marks."

"Stick out your tongue!"

I did, and then he asked me to remove my clothes, which I also did. As I stood naked and shivering on the tile floor, he poked my legs, pinched my ribs, thumped my back, pulled my ears, stared into my eyes, parted my hair, and raked it with his fingers, then examined my toes, looking for something only the Prophets knew.

"Put on this gown and wait in the next line," he said.

I slipped the gown over my head, then moved out of the line of naked men and boys, past the huge kettles where some of the emigrants' clothes were boiling. After a few moments he came up to me and said, "You have lice. You will not be allowed on the ship with lice."

The news hit me like a thunderclap, for Sandor had made me bathe every evening. "I can't have lice!" I exclaimed. "I don't itch!"

"Some people don't itch," he said.

"Boil my clothes," I said. "That will kill them. Shave my head too!"

"It's not just boiling your clothes," the man said. "They need a whole day to dry."

"I'll wear them wet!" I cried. "I've a ticket for the *Hamburg Queen* leaving tonight!"

In his detached voice he replied, "I would have to douse your garments in paraffin oil as well. That's ship's regulations. Then I would have to shave your head and wash your scalp three times. All this cannot be done by this afternoon. I have to examine everyone else in line first." He gave me an indifferent look, then said, "Of course, for forty-five marks I could put you in the 'Urgent' classification."

Forty-five marks! That was all the money I had; yet I asked, "If I paid, could I leave today, for sure?"

"Yes," he answered.

I took out the deutsche marks and handed them over. After glancing about, he pocketed the money quickly.

"Put these on," he ordered, giving me back my clothes.

"Aren't you going to boil them now?" I asked. "And what about my hair?"

Without answering, he took my passport, stamped it, showing I had passed the health inspection, and handed it back to me.

"I don't have lice, do I?" I asked in a voice of suppressed rage.

"Next!" he called.

I went out into the damp morning. I was very hungry, but now had not a single mark to buy food. Anger hung on me, heavy and gray as the drizzle. But as I walked along the docks, my anger gradually lifted. After all, I reasoned, I was at fault for so readily trusting him. Besides, I told myself, money or not, I am going to America! I am really going. And I am leaving tonight!

Wagons clattered past me, the horses' iron-shod hooves clacking loudly on the wet flagstones. Along the streets just before the estuary, shipping merchants were unrolling their salt-damp awnings. I wove my way around them, turned a corner, and came suddenly upon a wondrous sight. Sailing ships! As far as I could see through the mist, they lined the docks, their masts soaring like church steeples into the sky. How *big* ships are! I thought.

I ran along the wharf, checking each prow until I found the words *HAMBURG QUEEN*. When I looked up, I saw Zalman's boat made large. Its decks were filled with sailors working, and there came from it a constant, smacking sound of rope and sail.

I felt in my pocket again for the ticket. Safely there. The *Hamburg Queen* would not sail until seven that evening, and as I had nowhere to go until then, I roamed the waterfront. As the morning wore on, it became amazingly crowded. Drays and wheelbarrows, horses and people all jostled for the right of way. And though no one was traveling anywhere yet, everything that morning seemed in motion.

I leapt over piles of rope and hopped over crates to get past the crowds. At tables set up along the quays, peddlers of voyage provisions hawked their goods: dried beef, dried fruit, coffee, and rice. And weaving through the crowds with shrill songs came the peddlers of small things: lace and ribbon, candy, pocket mirrors, bread rolls, ivory combs, hairpins, and chestnuts.

In the late afternoon I took my place among the steerage passengers waiting to be let on the *Hamburg Queen*. A shipping-line official stood at the rail, checking off the names of the ticket holders as they came aboard. He must have been intent on catching anyone who hadn't paid, for beside him stood two burly crewmen, watching every soul who trudged up the slippery wet gangplank. The boarding took hours, but it was made pleasant by the merriment of well-wishers and the silly chanteys of some jobless sailors who sang for coins.

As soon as I was let on, I wanted to run about the ship as if it were my village. But I came to doors barred by heavy chains and so discovered that steerage passengers couldn't enter the first- and second-class compartments. We were confined to the main deck and the steerage quarters.

I turned from the chains and saw a swarm of people listening to a sailor who spoke to them in a loud, bored voice. He didn't talk so much as bark out words crudely in three or four different languages. I joined the edge of this crowd and found myself descending a rusty staircase to the steerage quarters, a dark inner space near the steering equipment. A flimsy, makeshift floor had been built on top of the cargo hold and beneath the main deck. It was this floor that held our bunks. The sailor led us through a gloomy maze of rooms, each lit only by a single, sooty lamp. He pointed to the metal beds, piled four bunks high, in which we 2,000 passengers were to sleep. The beds were narrow as coffins and crammed one on top of another, with less than an arm's length of space between each. All about these beds there was a stink as of a slop gully. The whole steerage section was like the dwelling of the Evil Eye; yet the sailor acted completely indifferent to the horror. He monotonously pointed out the vomiting buckets and the pits in the floor, which served as toilets. These pits made the stench of the bunkrooms so foul that I resolved to sleep up on deck. Fresh air, no matter how cold, seemed better to me.

When the sailor finished giving his tour, people in the crowd began to stake out their bunks. Passengers moved all about me, shouting to each other and pushing their way through with their bundles. The thin floor was slimy with bilge water that must have been used to clean it. So when I was pushed from behind by the great swell of people, I found myself skidding on this scummy floor, then landing on my stomach against a low bunk where I came face-to-face with a large rat. A young man lifted my arm to help me up, speaking to me in a language I had never heard before. His eyes were kind, but his breath was foul as wind from the netherworld. The smell of it along with the odor of excrement and rotting wood, all revolted me. I pushed my way up the stairs and outside to the main deck, where now I found a sea of ragged people. They had spread their bedding out everywhere and sat on it in disheveled heaps, looking much like their own bundles. Cries of babies mingled with the cries of gulls, and the darkening air seemed to hold a hundred languages.

I made my way over to the rail, passing a row of tall oak barrels. These were the herring barrels Sandor had told me about, and just the sight of them made my empty stomach grumble louder than ever. Sandor had said that every night crackers would be distributed and herring given to those who lined up for it. "Hurry to the barrels!" he had warned me. "Each night the shipping company rations the herring for the steerage passengers. If you're at the end of the line, you'll get nothing."

It was almost time to go. A shore gang of ship riggers came aboard to help hoist the sails. They climbed to the very top of the main mast and hovered there like angels. Pulling with all their might on the thick ropes, they raised the heavy sails. I watched in amazement as the canvas flew up, for it seemed there was a verst of it; yet their iron-strong arms made it quick work.

I stood at the rail until night fell. The sky and water grew black, stars sparkled near the earth, and the port of Hamburg shone with the yellow glow of lamplight. In the cold air I breathed in the damp smell of the dark ocean while I said my evening prayers. From somewhere a bell sounded, then the gangplank was pulled back. Leaning on the rail, I looked across the moonlit waters that led out to sea. Would I ever again see Mama, Papa, and Zalman? I wondered. Would I ever forget my life in Molovsk? A sudden sorrow came over me. I felt trapped—caught between hope and memory. "I want to leave," I heard myself say aloud, "yet I don't want to forget."

I gazed up at the stars, and after a while it was as if they cast my father's words down to me. "The closed circle has power, Mendel. Only the closed circle keeps us whole." Then somehow I knew that, just as sailing across a round earth, the traveler comes back full circle to where he started; as far as I went from Molovsk, I'd return, if only in my heart.

The crew did the last unfurling until all the sails were raised. Then fully expanded by the night wind, they were like the wings of some great bird readied for flight.

With a demon's groan the huge anchor was reeled up. We began to move. Freed from earth and thrust by wind, the ship cut powerfully through the dark water, its prow pointed toward America. I watched the lights on land until they all disappeared. Then I turned from the rail and hurried to the barrels.

Author's Note

Ven iz aroyzgekumen der gezets ven Yidishe zelner
Mir zenen zeh tseforn in eyntsikn vald
In eyntsikn vald zenen mir zeh tseforn
In eyntsige griber obn mir zeh geboltn.

When the law came down about Jewish soldiers
We all dispersed over the lonesome forests
Over the lonesome forests did we disperse
In lonesome pits did we hide ourselves.

Yiddish Folk Song

On August 26, 1827, Czar Nicholas I made a law that Jewish boys from age twelve to eighteen were to be conscripted for military service. The boys would receive religious and military training until the age of eighteen, then begin their twenty-five-year service. The children were called Cantonists because they were taken to live in military garrisons in distant "cantons," or provinces.

Jewish communities were held responsible for the supply of recruits and were fined heavily if they did not reach their quota. In 1851 the quota for Jewish boys was increased to percentages impossible to fill. Often, to make up for a lack of teenagers, communities were forced to send children as young as eight. The boys were taken to eastern provinces as far away from their homes in the Pale as possible. To reach their destination many were made to walk on foot from six months to a year.

The main purpose of the Cantonist battalions was to convert young Jews to Christianity. Conversion among the Cantonists was under the direct supervision of Czar Nicholas, who personally reviewed the Cantonist conversion lists each month. During his reign, more than 50,000 boys were taken. Under threat of torture, most of the children converted; yet nearly half did not survive the cruel treatment.

In 1855 Nicholas I died, and his son, Czar Alexander II, abolished child conscription. And so, after thirty years, the hated Cantonist system was ended.

Maxine Rose Schur has worked in a variety of media. In addition to her several books, she has written scripts for children's television and designed educational software.

One of her books, *Hannah Szenes: A Song of Light*, was a National Jewish Book Award Nominee and a National Council for the Social Studies Notable Book.

Ms. Schur lives in San Mateo, California, with her husband and two children.